This book of silly stories
and rhymes belongs to

_____

This is a Parragon Publishing Book
This edition published in 2003

Parragon Publishing
Queen Street House,
4 Queen Street,
Bath BA1 1HE, UK

Produced by
The Templar Company plc

Designed by Caroline Reeves

Printed and bound in Singapore
ISBN 0 75258 803 6

rocking horse, which he had entered in
one of the craft exhibits.

"You'll just have to not smile today," suggested
Grandma not very helpfully as she lay a large
pastry blanket over the fat wedges of juicy apple.
"Or talk," she added. Grandpa shrugged his
narrow shoulders and ambled over to his potting
shed, feeling fairly sorry for himself.

"Hmm, I wonder," said Grandma as she gazed
at the false teeth sitting on the edge of her table.
She picked them up thoughtfully, and then very
carefully and very neatly, she crimped the edge
of her apple pie with them. Grandpa stood in his
shed flicking a feather dust over the shiny
dappled neck of his fine rocking horse. He stood
back to admire his work. The horse was perfect
in every detail. A real leather saddle and bridle, a
silken mane and tail, neat glossy black hoofs and
two large brown eyes with wonderful long lashes.
Grandpa rubbed his bristly chin and frowned.

Something was missing, and he couldn't quite figure out what it was. The nostrils were finely carved and painted a fiery red, the muzzle was sanded to the smoothest finish, and a polished silver bit rested in the horse's mouth, but the mouth itself looked a little sad. Then Grandpa had a splendid idea.

He collected his teeth from the kitchen table and took them back to the shed. He glued them carefully into position. They were a perfect fit! Grandpa stood back and grinned a gummy grin, and the rocking horse grinned a toothy one.

"What a brilliant idea!" said Grandma. "Lottie and Jack are going to love him."

Grandma and Grandpa were taking Lottie and Jack, their grandchildren, to the fair. They didn't know about the rocking horse their grandpa had built for them—it was to be a very special surprise.

"Are you nearly ready?" asked Grandma, putting on her best straw hat, the one with the cherries on it.

"I think I'll wear my old straw boater," announced Grandpa heading for the stairs.

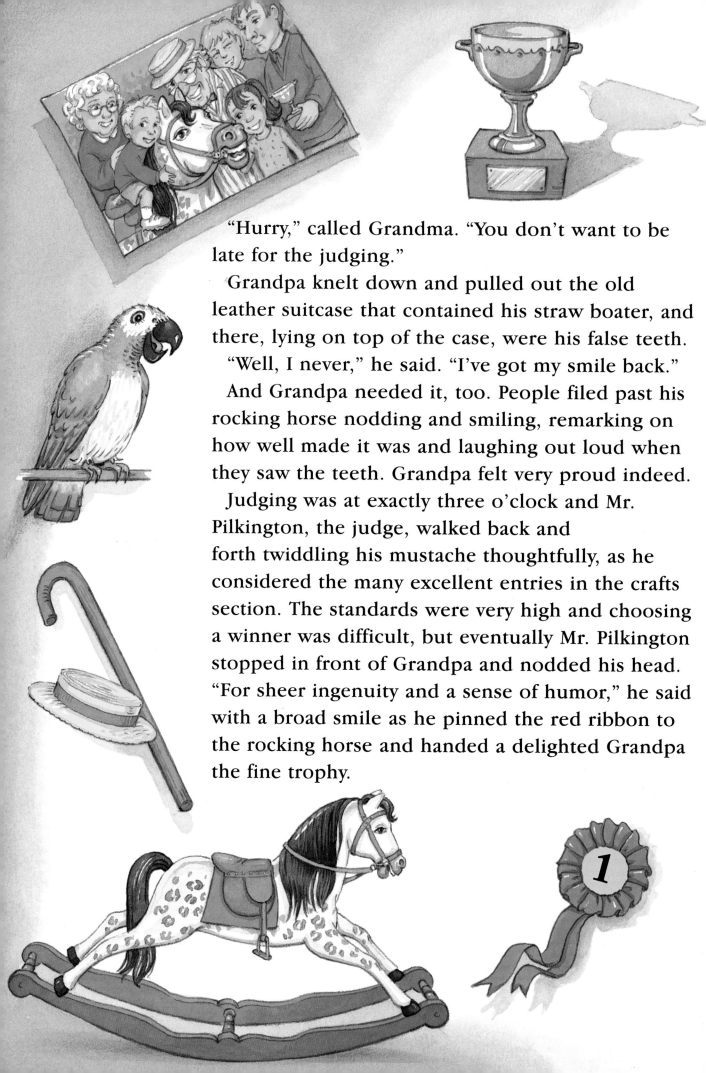

"Hurry," called Grandma. "You don't want to be late for the judging."

Grandpa knelt down and pulled out the old leather suitcase that contained his straw boater, and there, lying on top of the case, were his false teeth.

"Well, I never," he said. "I've got my smile back."

And Grandpa needed it, too. People filed past his rocking horse nodding and smiling, remarking on how well made it was and laughing out loud when they saw the teeth. Grandpa felt very proud indeed.

Judging was at exactly three o'clock and Mr. Pilkington, the judge, walked back and forth twiddling his mustache thoughtfully, as he considered the many excellent entries in the crafts section. The standards were very high and choosing a winner was difficult, but eventually Mr. Pilkington stopped in front of Grandpa and nodded his head. "For sheer ingenuity and a sense of humor," he said with a broad smile as he pinned the red ribbon to the rocking horse and handed a delighted Grandpa the fine trophy.

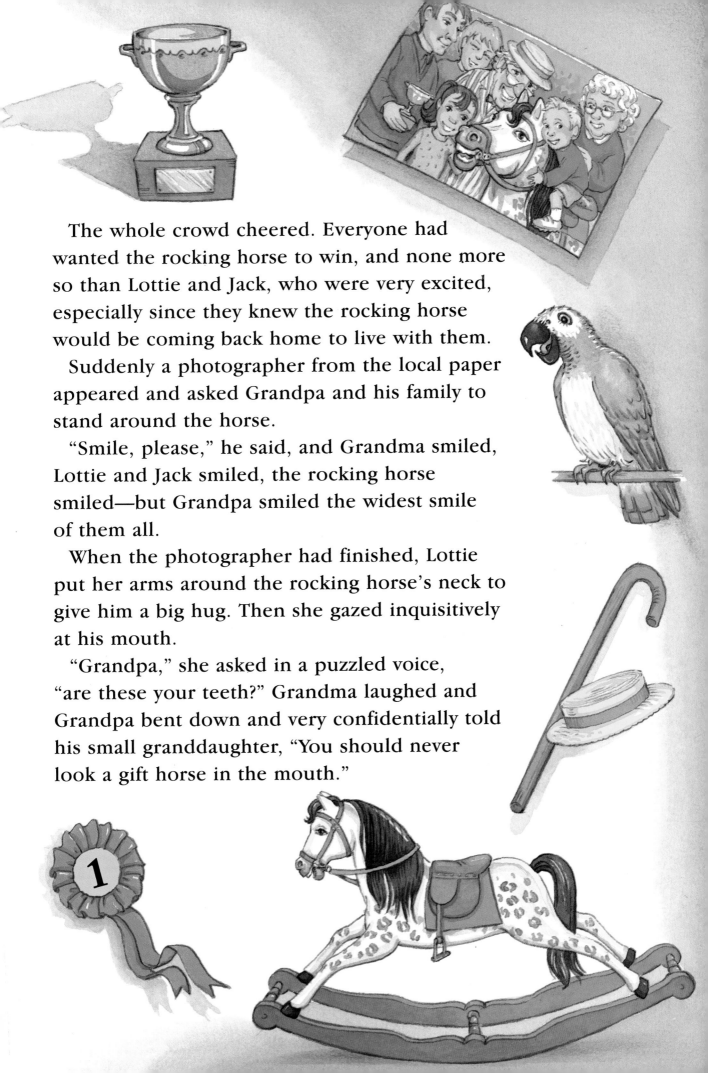

The whole crowd cheered. Everyone had wanted the rocking horse to win, and none more so than Lottie and Jack, who were very excited, especially since they knew the rocking horse would be coming back home to live with them.

Suddenly a photographer from the local paper appeared and asked Grandpa and his family to stand around the horse.

"Smile, please," he said, and Grandma smiled, Lottie and Jack smiled, the rocking horse smiled—but Grandpa smiled the widest smile of them all.

When the photographer had finished, Lottie put her arms around the rocking horse's neck to give him a big hug. Then she gazed inquisitively at his mouth.

"Grandpa," she asked in a puzzled voice, "are these your teeth?" Grandma laughed and Grandpa bent down and very confidentially told his small granddaughter, "You should never look a gift horse in the mouth."

My Funny Family

My aunt May's got a brain like a sieve—
She forgets where the things in her kitchen live.
There are plates in the fridge and chops in the drawers
Carrots in the mugs and hot dogs hung on doors.

My uncle Fred's got ears like cauliflowers—
He listens to the neighbors chat for hours and hours and hours
He can hear an ant whistling from a mile away or more,
And butterflies who flutter and ladybugs who snore!

My cousin Bob's got eyes like a hawk—
He can see all the way from Chicago to New York!
He says he can see planets orbiting in space,
And that the moon has a handlebar mustache upon its face.

My sister Sarah's got feet that love to dance—
She's danced from Perth to Benidorm, from Italy to France.
She dances in a dress trimmed with black and yellow lace,
Mom says she looks just like a bee and that it's a disgrace!

My brother Tom's got tricks up his sleeve—
He's got creepy things and spiders, and bugs to make you heave.
He once flicked a baked bean, which fell on Grandpa's head
And poor Grandpa didn't know until he went to bed!

My dog Jasper's got a ferocious appetite—
To see him gobbling up his food is really quite a sight.
He wolfs down spaghetti and when he's really feeling gross,
He'll polish off a cake and a pile of buttered toast!

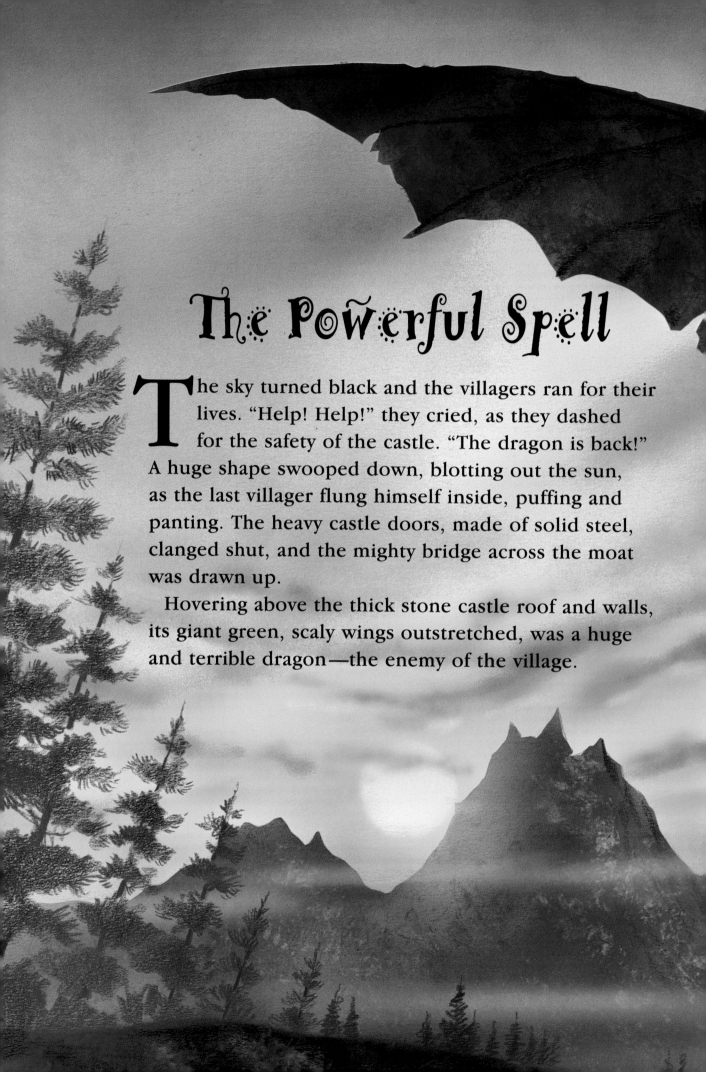

The Powerful Spell

The sky turned black and the villagers ran for their lives. "Help! Help!" they cried, as they dashed for the safety of the castle. "The dragon is back!" A huge shape swooped down, blotting out the sun, as the last villager flung himself inside, puffing and panting. The heavy castle doors, made of solid steel, clanged shut, and the mighty bridge across the moat was drawn up.

Hovering above the thick stone castle roof and walls, its giant green, scaly wings outstretched, was a huge and terrible dragon—the enemy of the village.

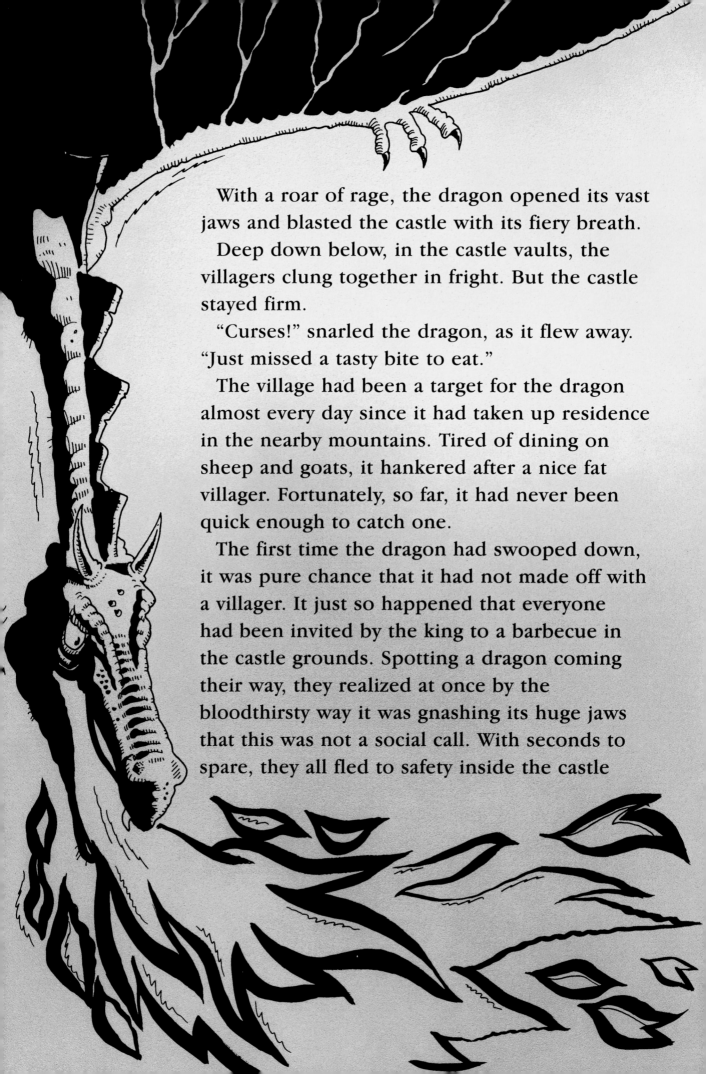

With a roar of rage, the dragon opened its vast jaws and blasted the castle with its fiery breath.

Deep down below, in the castle vaults, the villagers clung together in fright. But the castle stayed firm.

"Curses!" snarled the dragon, as it flew away. "Just missed a tasty bite to eat."

The village had been a target for the dragon almost every day since it had taken up residence in the nearby mountains. Tired of dining on sheep and goats, it hankered after a nice fat villager. Fortunately, so far, it had never been quick enough to catch one.

The first time the dragon had swooped down, it was pure chance that it had not made off with a villager. It just so happened that everyone had been invited by the king to a barbecue in the castle grounds. Spotting a dragon coming their way, they realized at once by the bloodthirsty way it was gnashing its huge jaws that this was not a social call. With seconds to spare, they all fled to safety inside the castle

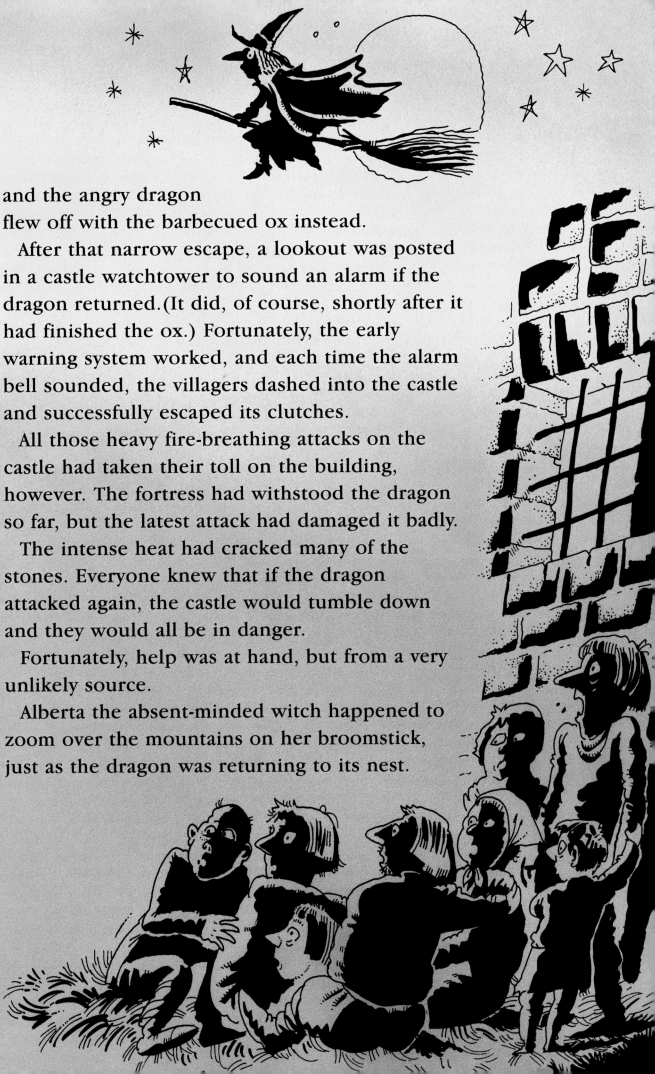

and the angry dragon
flew off with the barbecued ox instead.

After that narrow escape, a lookout was posted
in a castle watchtower to sound an alarm if the
dragon returned.(It did, of course, shortly after it
had finished the ox.) Fortunately, the early
warning system worked, and each time the alarm
bell sounded, the villagers dashed into the castle
and successfully escaped its clutches.

All those heavy fire-breathing attacks on the
castle had taken their toll on the building,
however. The fortress had withstood the dragon
so far, but the latest attack had damaged it badly.

The intense heat had cracked many of the
stones. Everyone knew that if the dragon
attacked again, the castle would tumble down
and they would all be in danger.

Fortunately, help was at hand, but from a very
unlikely source.

Alberta the absent-minded witch happened to
zoom over the mountains on her broomstick,
just as the dragon was returning to its nest.

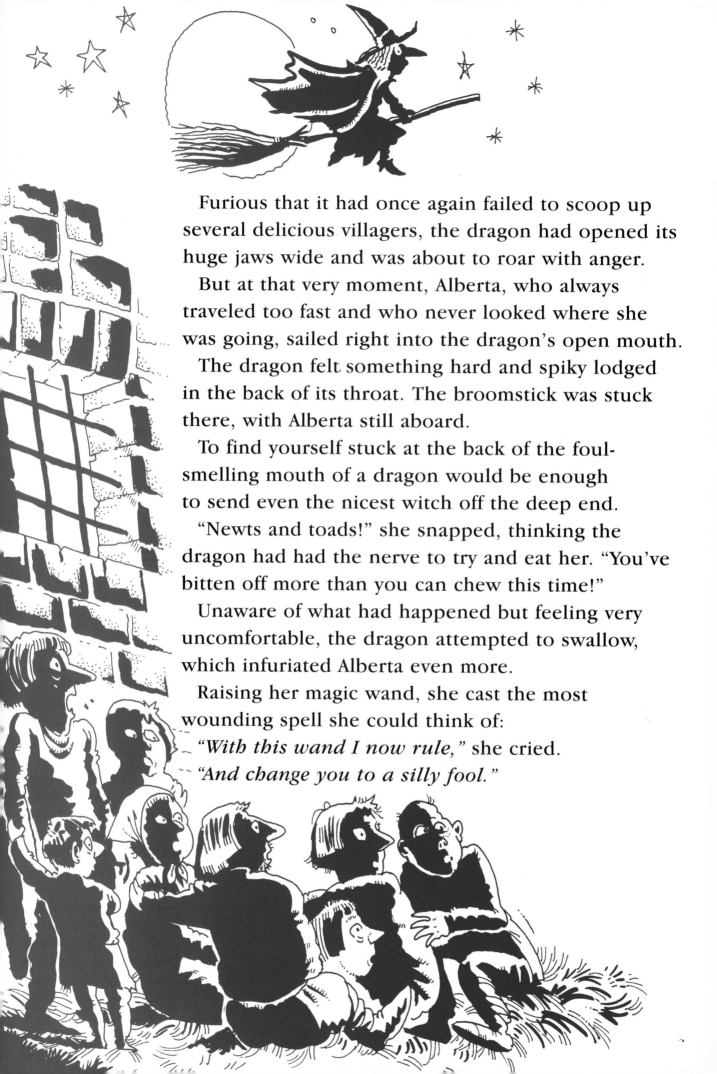

Furious that it had once again failed to scoop up several delicious villagers, the dragon had opened its huge jaws wide and was about to roar with anger.

But at that very moment, Alberta, who always traveled too fast and who never looked where she was going, sailed right into the dragon's open mouth.

The dragon felt something hard and spiky lodged in the back of its throat. The broomstick was stuck there, with Alberta still aboard.

To find yourself stuck at the back of the foul-smelling mouth of a dragon would be enough to send even the nicest witch off the deep end.

"Newts and toads!" she snapped, thinking the dragon had had the nerve to try and eat her. "You've bitten off more than you can chew this time!"

Unaware of what had happened but feeling very uncomfortable, the dragon attempted to swallow, which infuriated Alberta even more.

Raising her magic wand, she cast the most wounding spell she could think of:

"With this wand I now rule," she cried.
"And change you to a silly fool."

Then she conjured herself back to the comfort of her own home for a little rest and a restorative cup of slime tea.

Blissfully ignorant of the fact that a powerful spell had been cast upon it, the dragon returned to its nest. It was relieved that whatever had gotten stuck in its throat was no longer there, and had no idea that it had been a witch.

Later that day, however, it felt a little hungry.

"I'll show those villagers this time," the dragon promised itself, as it set off in search of tasty humans once again.

But little did the dragon realize exactly what kind of a show it would be putting on.

"Dragon ahoy!" shouted the look out sounding the alarm bell as the familiar giant black shape appeared in the sky.

The whole village was panic-stricken. They knew that the badly damaged castle wouldn't withstand another firebombing. If it tumbled down, the dragon would gobble them all up.

But there was nowhere else to run.
So, preparing themselves for the worst,
they shut themselves up inside it as usual.
Hidden well away from the huge holes in the
roof, they clung to each other for comfort and
prayed that somehow they would be saved.

And astonishingly enough, they were.

The dreadful beating noise made by the
dragon's vast wings came nearer and nearer. The
blue sky visible through the gaping holes in the
ceiling went black, as the dragon hovered
overhead. But the dreaded fiery jets of dragon
breath never came.

When the enchanted dragon drew a deep
breath and blew out with all its might, no sheets
of flame shot out. Instead, millions of sweet-
smelling flower petals fluttered downward
from its gaping jaws.

The villagers stared in amazement as pretty
petals floated through the holes above their
heads and gathered in drifts around their feet.

Scarcely able to believe its eyes either, the dragon gazed in horror at the beautiful blossoms heaped below.

Drawing a second, deeper breath, the dragon attempted to obliterate all that beauty with the biggest firebolt it had ever produced. But this time, showers of delicious candy rained down on the castle, fell through the cracks in the ceiling, and gathered in heaps on the floor around the villagers.

The furious dragon gave a loud roar of anguish, but Alberta's spell ensured that something just as silly as the flowers and candy emerged from its fearsome-looking jaws.

Instead of a spine-chilling bellow, the dragon started to yodel in a deep, rich baritone and found to its great embarrassment that it couldn't stop.

"I love you-ee-ou-ee-ou-ee-ou," it sang to the astonished villagers.

Inside the castle, everyone started to laugh. As the dragon continued to yodel a love song to them, they laughed even harder.

The dragon knew it was making a ridiculous spectacle of itself but thanks to Alberta's spell, it couldn't do anything about it.

Well, it could do something, the dragon realized. It could fly away and never come back.

And that is exactly what the dragon did.

"Good riddance to you, you silly fool," the king called after the dragon as it flew off over the castle walls as quickly as it could, still singing at the top of its voice.

Then everyone enjoyed a wonderful feast of candy, before they rebuilt the castle and lived happily ever after.

The Incredible Centipede

I'm not just an ordinary centipede,
  I live in a circus van,
  I know all the top performers,
And I have a wonderful plan...

We'll reach a town, and as the sun goes down,
The folks will crowd the tent;
With music to thrill, they'll pick up the bill
And read with astonishment:

"Star of the show in the ring tonight,
And we hope he does succeed,
Is the enterprising, most surprising,
Incredible Centipede!"

The curtains will part and out I'll dart
And shake a leg or six,
Then in spangled tights I'll scale the heights
To perform my amazing tricks.

I'll swing from the wire with a toehold catch
And fold my legs like a clown;
I'll pedal the bike with the balancing pole,
But I'll ride it upside down!

I'll fly though the air without a net—
They'll be standing on their seats.
The crowds will roar, they'll be calling for more
Of my incredible feats.

It will be so grand, in every land,
Royalty will want to be seen
Meeting the Incredible Centipede—
And I'll meet lots of kings and queens.

Silly Jill

There was once a girl named Jill Martin, and she always thought she knew best. Once, she took pity on a gorilla at her local zoo. She decided he would much rather live with her, than with his wife and babies in the jungle-like park that had been designed especially for them. So, one night, she crept into the zoo and lured him out of his enclosure with bunches of bananas, while his family was sleeping.

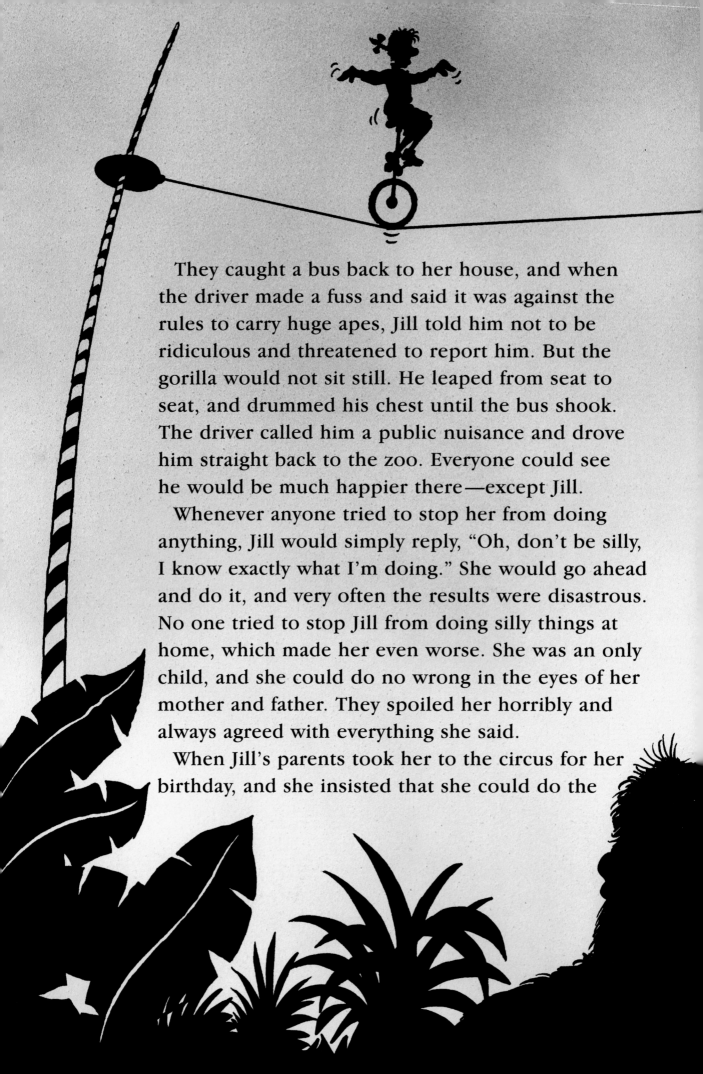

They caught a bus back to her house, and when the driver made a fuss and said it was against the rules to carry huge apes, Jill told him not to be ridiculous and threatened to report him. But the gorilla would not sit still. He leaped from seat to seat, and drummed his chest until the bus shook. The driver called him a public nuisance and drove him straight back to the zoo. Everyone could see he would be much happier there—except Jill.

Whenever anyone tried to stop her from doing anything, Jill would simply reply, "Oh, don't be silly, I know exactly what I'm doing." She would go ahead and do it, and very often the results were disastrous. No one tried to stop Jill from doing silly things at home, which made her even worse. She was an only child, and she could do no wrong in the eyes of her mother and father. They spoiled her horribly and always agreed with everything she said.

When Jill's parents took her to the circus for her birthday, and she insisted that she could do the

"Help!" they shouted, as one by one, they felt themselves being lifted off the floor.

A really extraordinary thing had happened. The spilled liquid had made something like grass grow out of the floor. Only, instead of growing slowly like grass usually does, this stuff was growing upward in leaps and bounds, like a meadow that had gone mad.

"Head for the door!" screamed the chemistry teacher, as the long waving carpet of grass carried them all up toward the ceiling. It was almost like being on a roller coaster.

So they all went, even Jill. They crawled across the narrow space that was still left as fast as they could, trying not to bang their heads on the lights, while the grassy carpet shot upward in a huge mass.

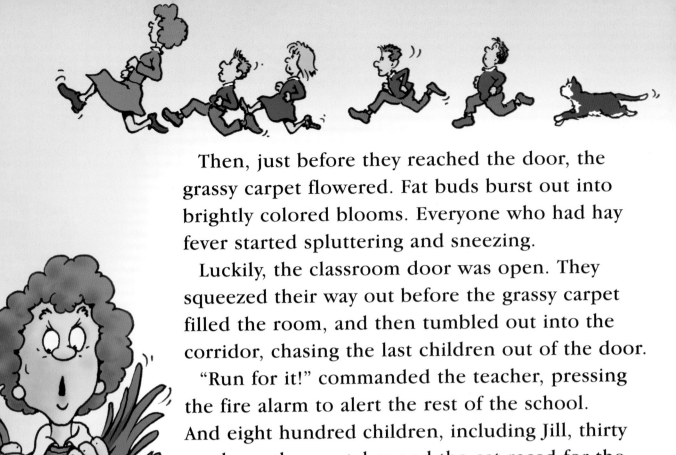

Then, just before they reached the door, the grassy carpet flowered. Fat buds burst out into brightly colored blooms. Everyone who had hay fever started spluttering and sneezing.

Luckily, the classroom door was open. They squeezed their way out before the grassy carpet filled the room, and then tumbled out into the corridor, chasing the last children out of the door.

"Run for it!" commanded the teacher, pressing the fire alarm to alert the rest of the school. And eight hundred children, including Jill, thirty teachers, the caretaker and the cat raced for the safety of the school yard, just before the school was completely swallowed up by a carpet of grass.

It took every fire fighter in town a week to cut the carpet down, and for months afterward it still sprouted the occasional flower.

The school had to be closed, of course, while the giant carpet was cut, mowed, rolled, and finally brought under control. The principal was furious with Jill when she heard how it had all started.

"Your silly, thoughtless behavior could have destroyed this school and everyone in it," she told her. "I hope this has taught you a lesson and you know now that you do not always know better than anyone else."

Fortunately for Jill—and the school—it had taught her a lesson that she never forgot. From that dreadful day on, she stopped insisting she knew best, and to everyone's relief, there were no more disasters.

In fact, Jill's terrible mistake turned out to be a fantastic opportunity for the school. A high-ranking army officer heard about Jill's silly experiment and the amazing result. He decided that a quick-growing carpet would be an excellent weapon. He paid the school a lot of money for the details of Jill's purple mixture. This meant that the school was able to build a swimming pool, ice rink and bowling alley for the whole town to use. And it wasn't long before Jill mended her ways and really did become a star pupil—but everyone still knew her as Silly Jill!

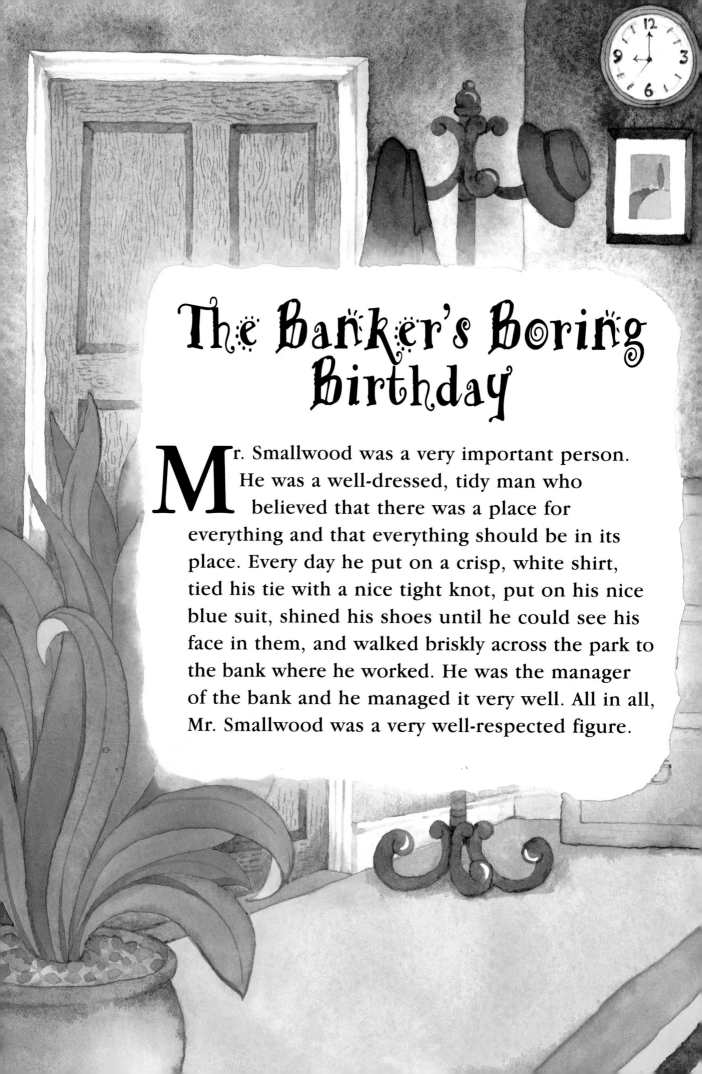

The Banker's Boring Birthday

Mr. Smallwood was a very important person. He was a well-dressed, tidy man who believed that there was a place for everything and that everything should be in its place. Every day he put on a crisp, white shirt, tied his tie with a nice tight knot, put on his nice blue suit, shined his shoes until he could see his face in them, and walked briskly across the park to the bank where he worked. He was the manager of the bank and he managed it very well. All in all, Mr. Smallwood was a very well-respected figure.

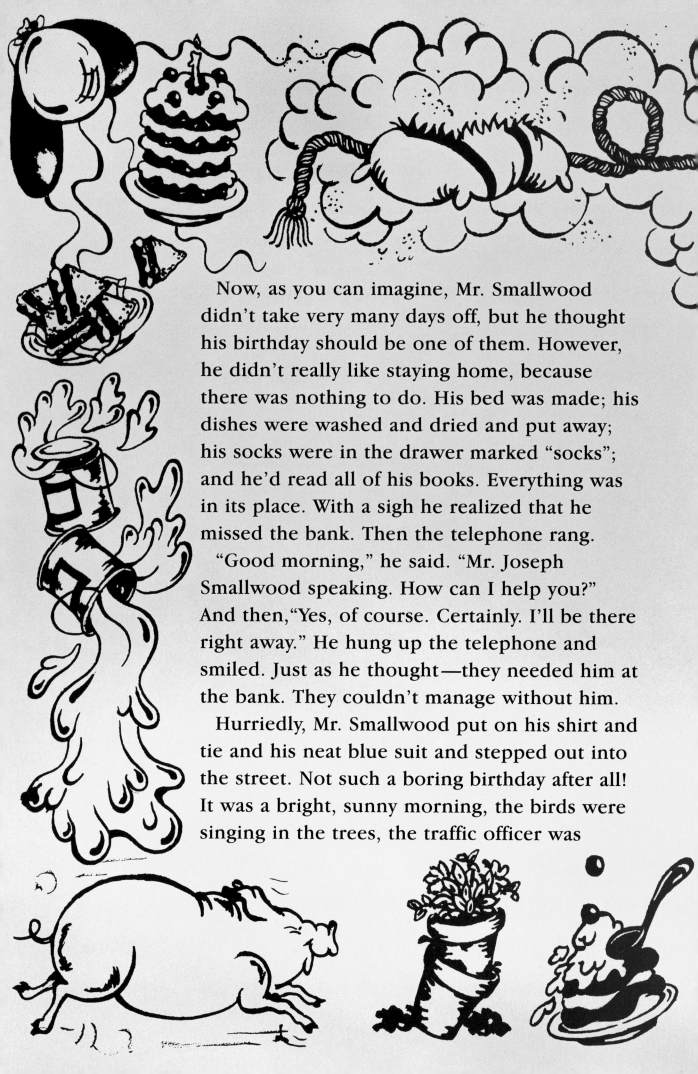

Now, as you can imagine, Mr. Smallwood didn't take very many days off, but he thought his birthday should be one of them. However, he didn't really like staying home, because there was nothing to do. His bed was made; his dishes were washed and dried and put away; his socks were in the drawer marked "socks"; and he'd read all of his books. Everything was in its place. With a sigh he realized that he missed the bank. Then the telephone rang.

"Good morning," he said. "Mr. Joseph Smallwood speaking. How can I help you?" And then, "Yes, of course. Certainly. I'll be there right away." He hung up the telephone and smiled. Just as he thought—they needed him at the bank. They couldn't manage without him.

Hurriedly, Mr. Smallwood put on his shirt and tie and his neat blue suit and stepped out into the street. Not such a boring birthday after all! It was a bright, sunny morning, the birds were singing in the trees, the traffic officer was

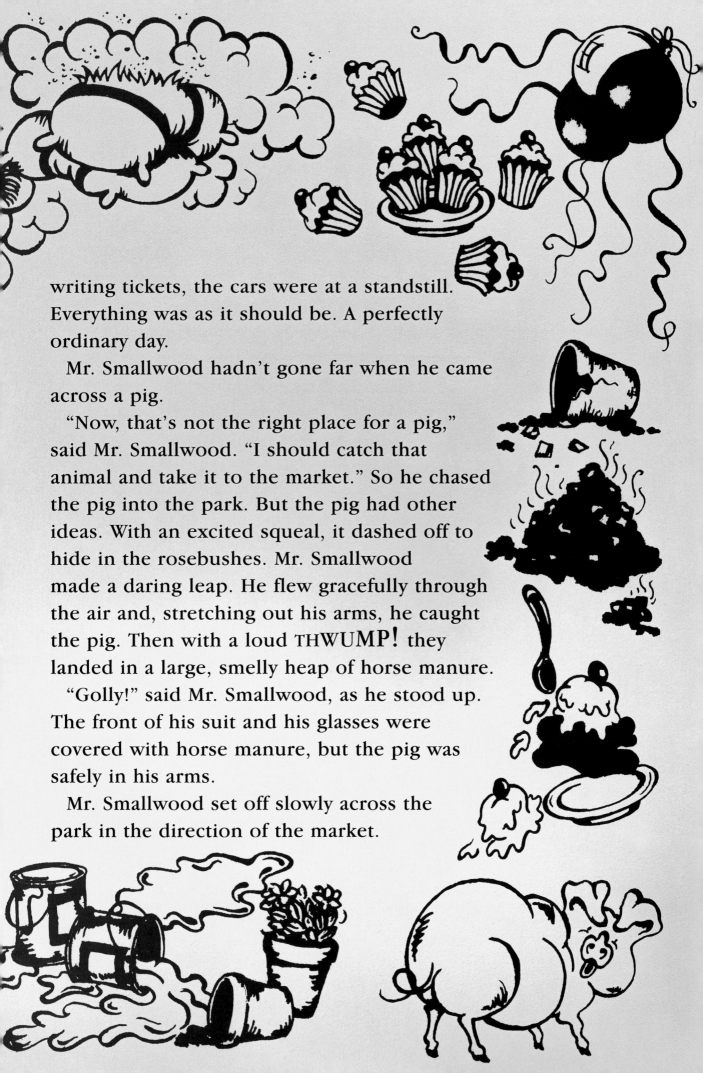

writing tickets, the cars were at a standstill.
Everything was as it should be. A perfectly
ordinary day.

Mr. Smallwood hadn't gone far when he came
across a pig.

"Now, that's not the right place for a pig,"
said Mr. Smallwood. "I should catch that
animal and take it to the market." So he chased
the pig into the park. But the pig had other
ideas. With an excited squeal, it dashed off to
hide in the rosebushes. Mr. Smallwood
made a daring leap. He flew gracefully through
the air and, stretching out his arms, he caught
the pig. Then with a loud THWUMP! they
landed in a large, smelly heap of horse manure.

"Golly!" said Mr. Smallwood, as he stood up.
The front of his suit and his glasses were
covered with horse manure, but the pig was
safely in his arms.

Mr. Smallwood set off slowly across the
park in the direction of the market.

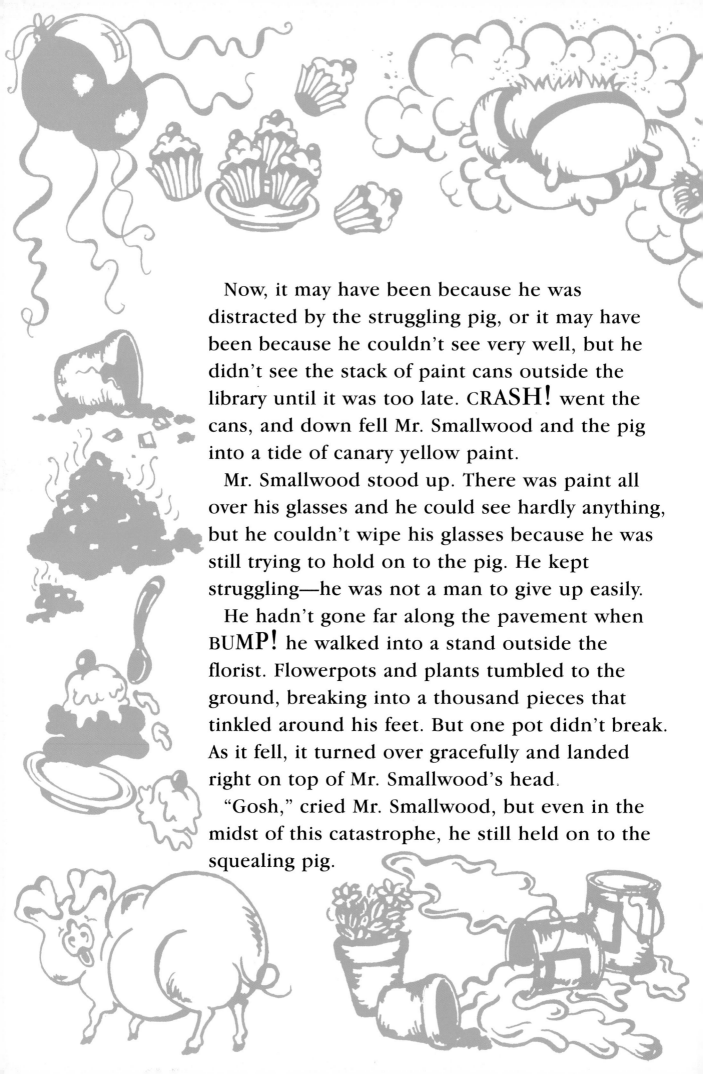

Now, it may have been because he was distracted by the struggling pig, or it may have been because he couldn't see very well, but he didn't see the stack of paint cans outside the library until it was too late. CRASH! went the cans, and down fell Mr. Smallwood and the pig into a tide of canary yellow paint.

Mr. Smallwood stood up. There was paint all over his glasses and he could see hardly anything, but he couldn't wipe his glasses because he was still trying to hold on to the pig. He kept struggling—he was not a man to give up easily.

He hadn't gone far along the pavement when BUMP! he walked into a stand outside the florist. Flowerpots and plants tumbled to the ground, breaking into a thousand pieces that tinkled around his feet. But one pot didn't break. As it fell, it turned over gracefully and landed right on top of Mr. Smallwood's head.

"Gosh," cried Mr. Smallwood, but even in the midst of this catastrophe, he still held on to the squealing pig.

emperor's startled and alarmed face, was an elephant's long, twisty trunk!

Well, what a commotion broke out! At first the courtiers were stunned into silence. Then there was a great hullaballoo, since, not knowing whether to laugh or cry, they bombarded the secretly astonished and horrified court jester with questions. I say secretly, because although his magic skills were not much good, he was a complete professional, and was not about to let on for one moment that this was anything but what he had intended. He was also well aware that emperors are notoriously easy to fool, and luckily for him, this one was no exception.

"Your Majesty!" he exclaimed, bowing low. "I am delighted to report a complete success! What a noble and distinctive nose, what an exceptionally unique profile. Doesn't he look marvelous?" The court jester turned to the courtiers, who, anxious not to offend the emperor, all loudly declared their approval!

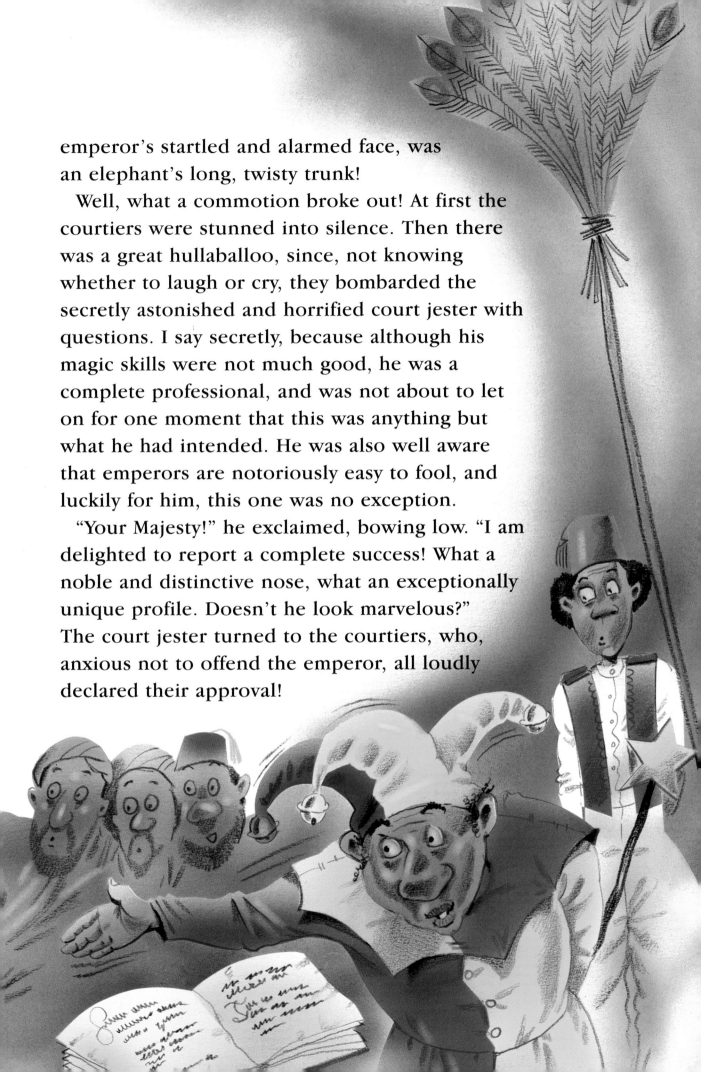

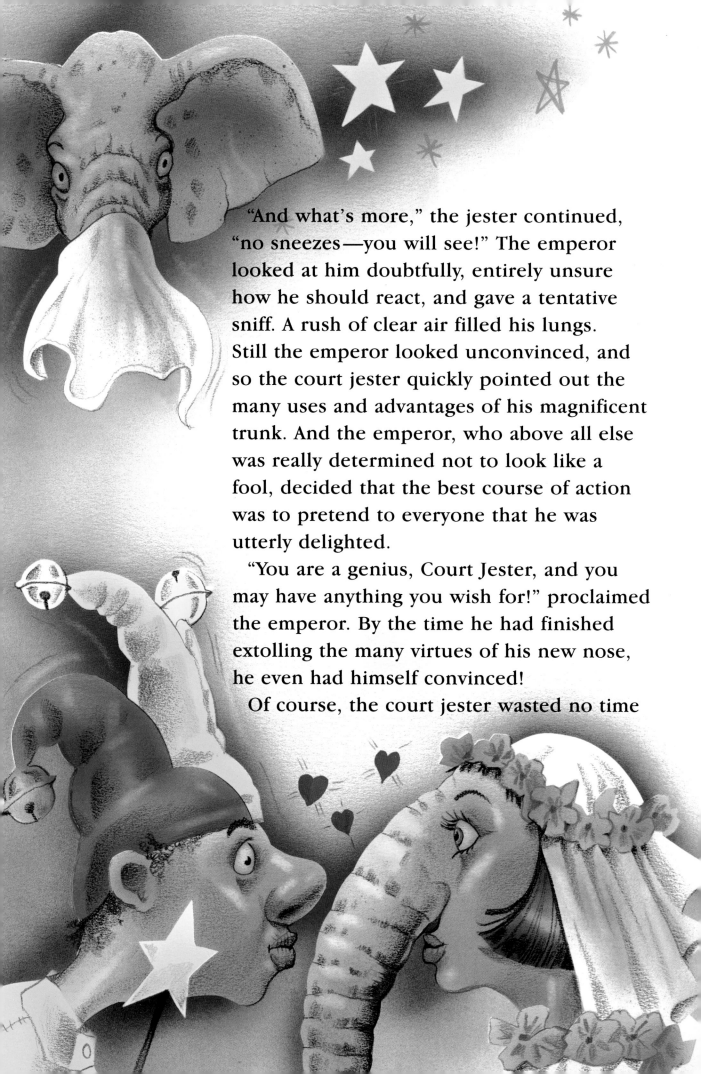

"And what's more," the jester continued, "no sneezes—you will see!" The emperor looked at him doubtfully, entirely unsure how he should react, and gave a tentative sniff. A rush of clear air filled his lungs. Still the emperor looked unconvinced, and so the court jester quickly pointed out the many uses and advantages of his magnificent trunk. And the emperor, who above all else was really determined not to look like a fool, decided that the best course of action was to pretend to everyone that he was utterly delighted.

"You are a genius, Court Jester, and you may have anything you wish for!" proclaimed the emperor. By the time he had finished extolling the many virtues of his new nose, he even had himself convinced!

Of course, the court jester wasted no time

in claiming the fair Bella's hand, and the wedding was arranged to take place at once. Bella was summoned from her bedchamber, where she had rushed to change into her wedding dress and veil as soon as the court jester had started his spell. The emperor looked on with resignation as his beloved daughter became the jester's blushing bride. And blushing she was….

"You may now kiss the bride!" declared the minister. The court jester eagerly lifted Bella's veil, closed his eyes, puckered up, and planted a big, sloppy kiss on her rough, wrinkled, and rather hairy… trunk!

Well! Like father, like daughter, I guess! Oh, and as for the elephant, he never did figure out what happened to his trunk, or why he was left with the most terrible c-c-c-c-cold! Aaaachoo!

A Shipful of Fun

It was a wild, stormy night. Windows rattled and garbage can lids clattered down the narrow . streets. Poppy sat wide awake in her bed, listening to the wind howling and the crashing waves. She wondered about the poor seagulls— where would they go on a night like this? Suddenly, her room was filled with bright orange light. A flare! Something was happening at sea! Poppy woke her father and they rushed down to the beach, pulling on their coats. People were appearing from everywhere and there was an air of anticipation as they all gathered on the beach—Poppy had the feeling it would be an eventful night.

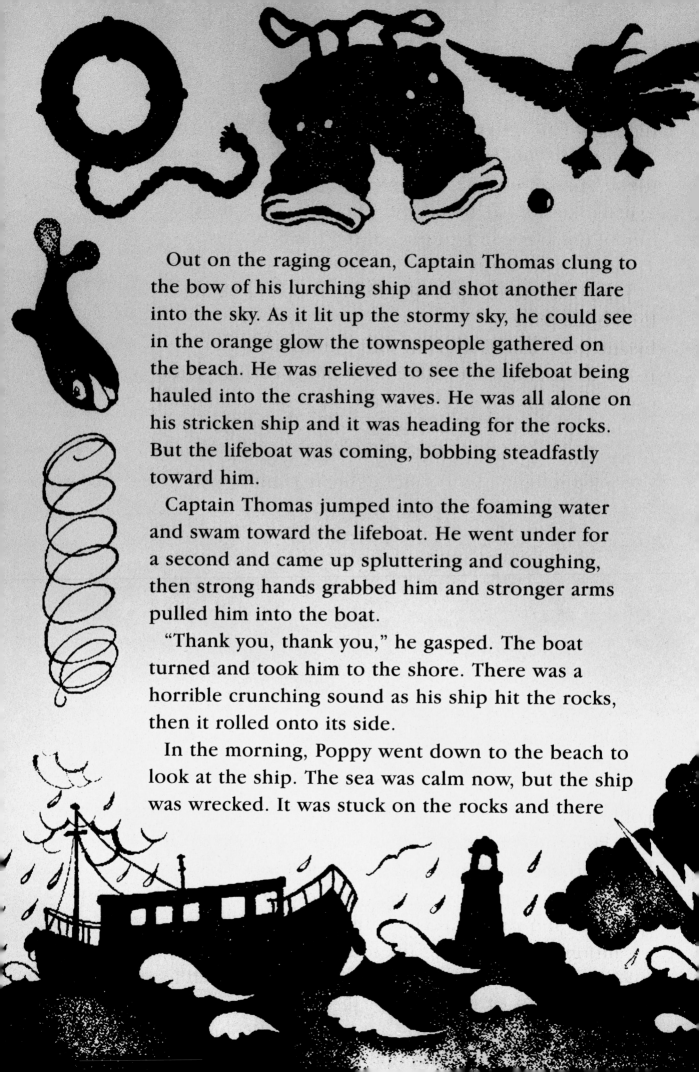

Out on the raging ocean, Captain Thomas clung to
the bow of his lurching ship and shot another flare
into the sky. As it lit up the stormy sky, he could see
in the orange glow the townspeople gathered on
the beach. He was relieved to see the lifeboat being
hauled into the crashing waves. He was all alone on
his stricken ship and it was heading for the rocks.
But the lifeboat was coming, bobbing steadfastly
toward him.

Captain Thomas jumped into the foaming water
and swam toward the lifeboat. He went under for
a second and came up spluttering and coughing,
then strong hands grabbed him and stronger arms
pulled him into the boat.

"Thank you, thank you," he gasped. The boat
turned and took him to the shore. There was a
horrible crunching sound as his ship hit the rocks,
then it rolled onto its side.

In the morning, Poppy went down to the beach to
look at the ship. The sea was calm now, but the ship
was wrecked. It was stuck on the rocks and there

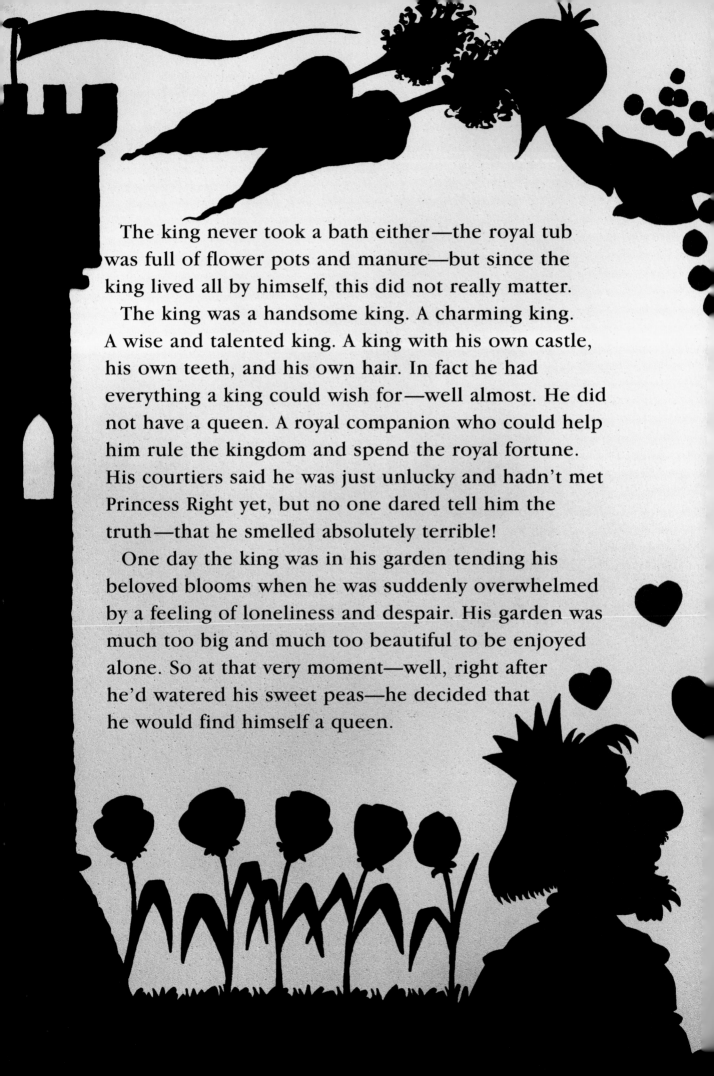

The king never took a bath either—the royal tub was full of flower pots and manure—but since the king lived all by himself, this did not really matter.

The king was a handsome king. A charming king. A wise and talented king. A king with his own castle, his own teeth, and his own hair. In fact he had everything a king could wish for—well almost. He did not have a queen. A royal companion who could help him rule the kingdom and spend the royal fortune. His courtiers said he was just unlucky and hadn't met Princess Right yet, but no one dared tell him the truth—that he smelled absolutely terrible!

One day the king was in his garden tending his beloved blooms when he was suddenly overwhelmed by a feeling of loneliness and despair. His garden was much too big and much too beautiful to be enjoyed alone. So at that very moment—well, right after he'd watered his sweet peas—he decided that he would find himself a queen.

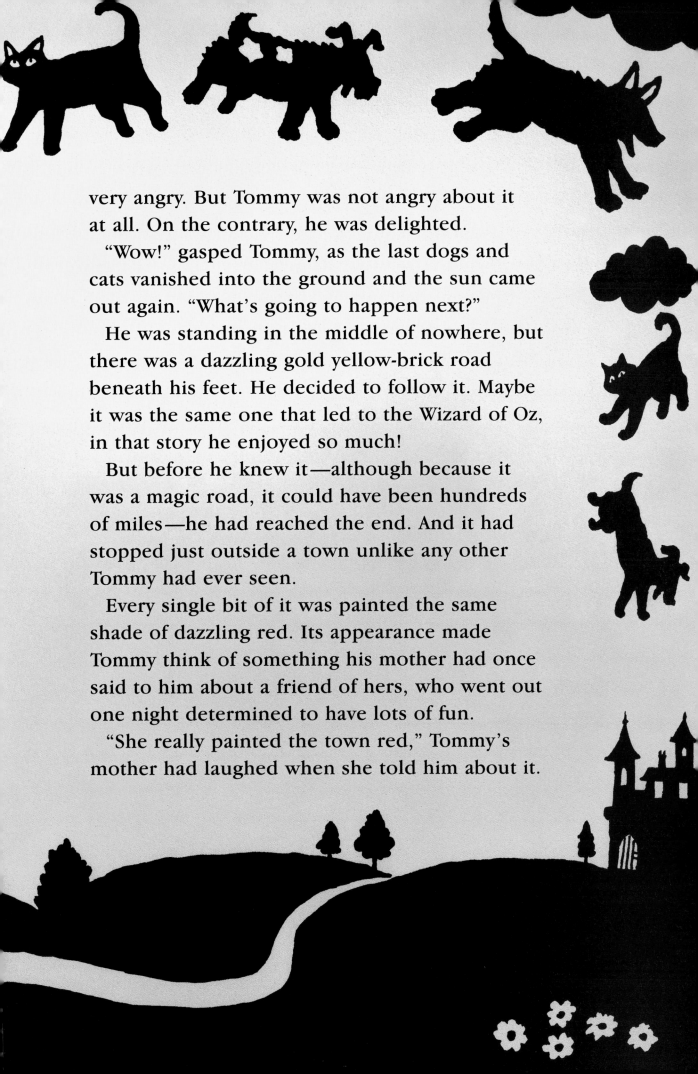

very angry. But Tommy was not angry about it at all. On the contrary, he was delighted.

"Wow!" gasped Tommy, as the last dogs and cats vanished into the ground and the sun came out again. "What's going to happen next?"

He was standing in the middle of nowhere, but there was a dazzling gold yellow-brick road beneath his feet. He decided to follow it. Maybe it was the same one that led to the Wizard of Oz, in that story he enjoyed so much!

But before he knew it—although because it was a magic road, it could have been hundreds of miles—he had reached the end. And it had stopped just outside a town unlike any other Tommy had ever seen.

Every single bit of it was painted the same shade of dazzling red. Its appearance made Tommy think of something his mother had once said to him about a friend of hers, who went out one night determined to have lots of fun.

"She really painted the town red," Tommy's mother had laughed when she told him about it.

Tommy knew that meant she'd had a really good time, not that she'd spent the whole night with a paintbrush in her hand. That wouldn't have been much fun! Looking at this town, however, it looked as if someone had done precisely that.

The fact that absolutely everything, even the trees and flowers, were the same shade of red was not the only weird thing about the town. It also seemed to be completely deserted.

Or was it? Out of the corner of his eye, Tommy thought he saw moving figures. It was very spooky.

"This looks like a ghost town," thought Tommy.

He was right. It was full of ghosts. But these ghosts were frightened of him!

"You're not going to haunt us, are you?" a friendly phantom plucked up courage to ask Tommy. "We've heard that humans go around wailing and clanking chains."

Tommy was about to reply, "No, that's what ghosts do!" but he realized that everything was backwards here. So he just smiled and said that of course he wouldn't.

However, Tommy was feeling a little nervous himself, and he wanted to explore the strange new world.

"I'm tired of seeing red," he told the phantom. "It's driving me up the wall."

His words came true. A moment later, Tommy found himself standing on top of a great wall that went all around the town.

"I've been told that walls have ears," Tommy told it, jokingly. "Maybe you do! You are totally unlike any wall I've ever met."

"You don't have to shout!" the wall retorted, proving that it did have excellent hearing.

Just then, a loud and very unexpected "Oink" sounded above Tommy's head, followed by a succession of noisy grunts. Tommy looked up and was amazed to see a herd of pigs flying toward him. They had

made a V-shaped formation, like geese, but squealed rather than honked as they flew, propelling themselves along by flapping their huge pink ears.

"Well, if it can rain cats and dogs, there's no reason why pigs shouldn't fly!" Tommy laughed. "Maybe we could even hitch a ride on the back of one."

"Come on!" he shouted to the friendly ghost.

They both rose to the occasion—in the wonderful world of "If", you really can—and floated upward to join the flying pigs.

"You want to go the whole hog, do you?" squealed a large black-and-white sow with ten spotted piglets fluttering along behind her. "Well, jump aboard."

She flew them down to a beach and then took off again.

"I must keep up with the others," she grunted, "in order to save my bacon!"

Tommy and the ghost made for the inviting blue ocean. Strangely, it seemed to be singing. As Tommy got closer, he realized it was the sound of many different singsong voices, all talking at once but very softly. He couldn't hear what they were saying to him, but it all sounded very flattering.

"I think they must be whispering sweet nothings to me," Tommy laughed.

"Whhoo-oo, I love sweet nothings!" the ghost moaned with pleasure. "I'll sit here for a while and fish for compliments."

He produced a fishing net out of thin air and dipped it into the ocean. But all he got for his efforts, was a sackful of trouble.

This being "If," however, it was not an imaginary sack full of imaginary troubles, it was the real thing.

"We'll just have to wing it now," Tommy said anxiously, fearing the worst as the bulging bag was lifted out, dripping with water and looking like a real load of problems. He suddenly felt himself going up in the world again. But this time it was as if he was bouncing off an extra springy trampoline.

"We *are* winging it!" Tommy called to the phantom delightedly. "We're really flying."

But when he finally came down to earth again with a bump, there was no sign of the friendly ghost. In fact, he was right back where he had started—in bed.

And Tommy did wonder if he might not have dreamed the whole thing. Just in case, he quickly looked out the window to see if it was still raining cats and dogs— but there was only a clear blue sky!

When Dreams Come True

There's a town called Corking, not far from here,
Where dreams come true every hundred years.
"That sounds terrific," I hear you cry,
But it isn't so great, and I'll tell you why.

There was a girl named Mag with feet so large
That people cried, "They're as big as a barge!"
She wished for little feet, small and round,
But when she got them, she kept falling down.

A man named Sam wanted a sea of beer,
And that's what he got—right up to his ears.
You'd think a sea of beer would satisfy him,
But the trouble was, he couldn't swim.

There was a girl named Lucy who climbed into trees,
Because she wanted to talk to the birds and bees,
But the sparrows and starlings all wanted to chat,
And Lucy just couldn't compete with all that.

There was a boy named Arnie who wished he was strong.
His dream came true, but it didn't last long.
Everything he touched just snapped into two,
And in no time at all, he had run out of glue.

So you see what I'm getting at in this little rhyme,
You can figure it out, if you give it some time.
Beware what you wish for— and I'm talking to you—
You never know, it might come true!

Follow the Leader

Sasha the sheep lived, as most sheep do, in a large field with a whole bunch of other sheep, carefully watched over by the farmer and his trusty sheepdogs. The farmer seemed to be a reasonable fellow, who made sure they had everything they needed, but the sheepdogs were a surly, miserable bunch, always barking out their orders and expecting to be obeyed. This suited the other sheep pretty well, because they were not good at thinking for themselves. But Sasha… well, Sasha was… different.

Ever since she was a tiny lamb her mother had known she would not grow up to be an ordinary sheep. While the other little lambs frolicked gaily in the meadow, chasing each other and gamboling nimbly, Sasha strode back and forth at the edge of the field, muttering fiercely under her breath. When she grew older she would sit for hours with her head buried in a book, or scribbling furiously on little pieces of paper which she hid in the bushes. Other times she went missing altogether, which sent her mother into a frenzy, convinced she had been carried off by a wolf. Then she would find her, propped upside down behind a tree. Meditating, Sasha called it. Getting in touch with her inner self. And it seemed that Sasha had an awful lot of self to get in touch with. The teenage years were the worst—she would stomp around the field, in one of her "moods," glowering at anyone who tried to follow her.

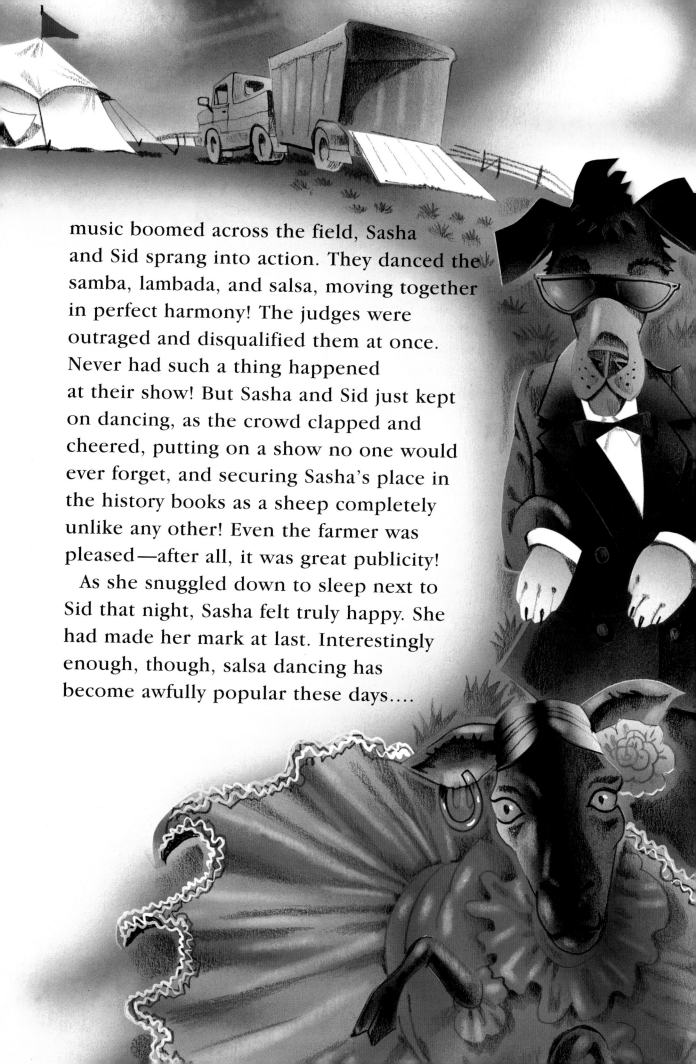

music boomed across the field, Sasha
and Sid sprang into action. They danced the
samba, lambada, and salsa, moving together
in perfect harmony! The judges were
outraged and disqualified them at once.
Never had such a thing happened
at their show! But Sasha and Sid just kept
on dancing, as the crowd clapped and
cheered, putting on a show no one would
ever forget, and securing Sasha's place in
the history books as a sheep completely
unlike any other! Even the farmer was
pleased—after all, it was great publicity!

As she snuggled down to sleep next to
Sid that night, Sasha felt truly happy. She
had made her mark at last. Interestingly
enough, though, salsa dancing has
become awfully popular these days....

The Sensible Tax

"The bridge is falling down," said the transportation minister.

"We need more golf balls," said the sports minister.

The prime minister didn't look up from his papers, but waved his hand wearily and said with a sigh, "Go to the treasury and get what you need."

"The treasury is empty, sir. There's not a single penny left."

"I don't believe it," said the prime minister. "It was full last week."

"I think we spent it all on that tunnel under the sea, sir," said the second minister. "You know, the one we can't find the entrance to."

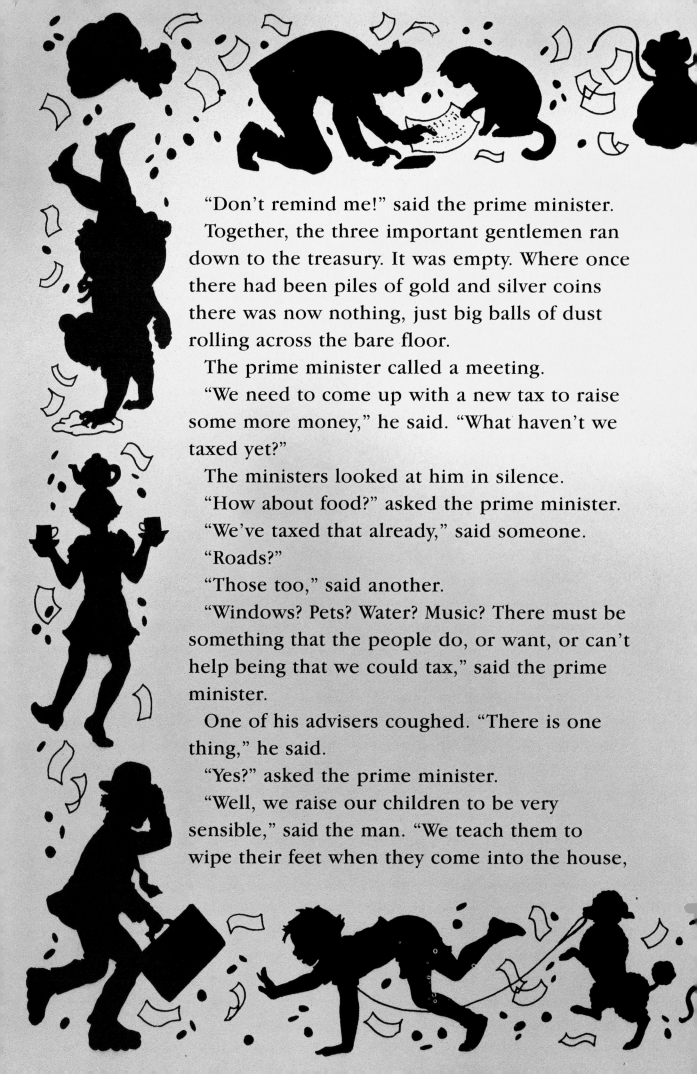

"Don't remind me!" said the prime minister.

Together, the three important gentlemen ran down to the treasury. It was empty. Where once there had been piles of gold and silver coins there was now nothing, just big balls of dust rolling across the bare floor.

The prime minister called a meeting.

"We need to come up with a new tax to raise some more money," he said. "What haven't we taxed yet?"

The ministers looked at him in silence.

"How about food?" asked the prime minister.

"We've taxed that already," said someone.

"Roads?"

"Those too," said another.

"Windows? Pets? Water? Music? There must be something that the people do, or want, or can't help being that we could tax," said the prime minister.

One of his advisers coughed. "There is one thing," he said.

"Yes?" asked the prime minister.

"Well, we raise our children to be very sensible," said the man. "We teach them to wipe their feet when they come into the house,

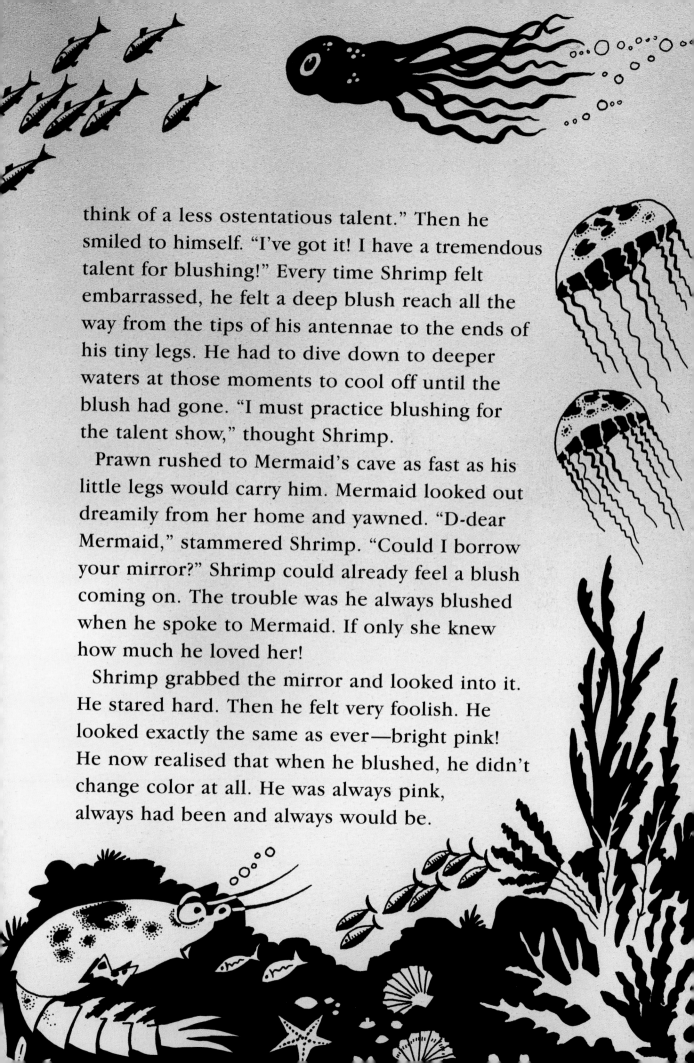

think of a less ostentatious talent." Then he smiled to himself. "I've got it! I have a tremendous talent for blushing!" Every time Shrimp felt embarrassed, he felt a deep blush reach all the way from the tips of his antennae to the ends of his tiny legs. He had to dive down to deeper waters at those moments to cool off until the blush had gone. "I must practice blushing for the talent show," thought Shrimp.

Prawn rushed to Mermaid's cave as fast as his little legs would carry him. Mermaid looked out dreamily from her home and yawned. "D-dear Mermaid," stammered Shrimp. "Could I borrow your mirror?" Shrimp could already feel a blush coming on. The trouble was he always blushed when he spoke to Mermaid. If only she knew how much he loved her!

Shrimp grabbed the mirror and looked into it. He stared hard. Then he felt very foolish. He looked exactly the same as ever—bright pink! He now realised that when he blushed, he didn't change color at all. He was always pink, always had been and always would be.

Mermaid gazed at Shrimp from under her lovely lashes. "What's up, Shrimp?" she drawled. "You look upset." "Oh, n-nothing," replied Shrimp, as he handed her the mirror. She was looking at him with her clear blue eyes and Shrimp couldn't think of anything to say. "Must run. Lots to do," he gulped as he swam off. "Ah, he is sweet," thought Mermaid wistfully, as she went back into her cave.

Shrimp was sad. The talent show would be starting soon, and he had nothing to offer. As Shrimp peeked out through the weeds, he could see that the ocean was alive with excited and purposeful activity. A group of clams were practicing opening and closing their shells in sequence. Anglerfish was unscrewing the light at the end of his fishing rod and putting a glitter ball in its place. Then Shrimp spotted Cool Daddy Squid with a nervous-looking young starfish at his side. "You're gonna be the greatest!" he heard Cool Daddy whisper to the starfish.

looked up. Mermaid was swimming toward him with tears in her eyes. She rushed up onto the stage and kissed and hugged him joyfully. "Thank you, Shrimp!" she cried. "You have played the most beautiful music on my harp that I have ever heard." The crowd cheered. Shrimp blushed.

"I suppose you could call it a hidden talent," he said.

The Planet Where Time Goes Backwards

Far beyond our solar system,
In the outer reaches of space,
There's a planet where time goes backwards,
And it's the most peculiar place.

A place where birds climb into their shells,
And leaves flutter up to the trees,
Clouds suck rain from out of the ground,
And rivers flow out of the seas.

Cooks wash the dishes before the meal starts
And unpeel potatoes, I'm told.
Your dinner goes into the oven,
And comes out nice and cold.

Construction workers start with a house
And take it apart brick by brick.
At lunchtime they spit out their sandwiches.
(It looks like they're being sick!)

At gas pumps they take the fuel out of cars,
And football's not much of a laugh:
The game ends with both teams at zero,
And they start by taking a bath.

You know something bad's going to happen,
When somebody starts to cry.
But the people get younger each day,
And they greet you by saying "Goodbye."

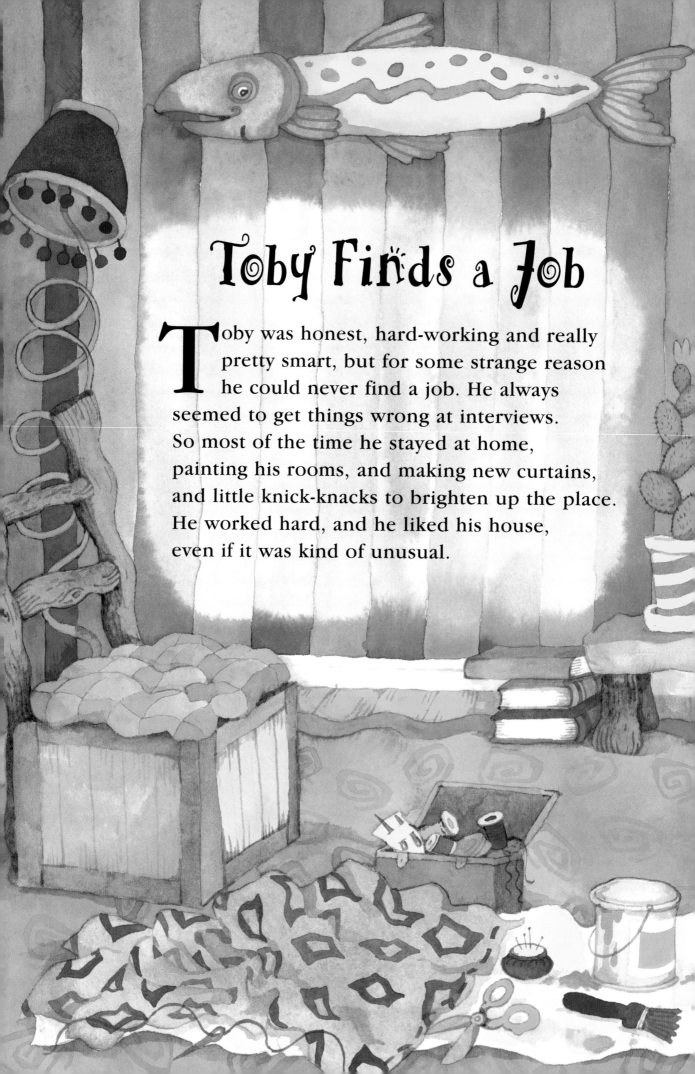

Toby Finds a Job

Toby was honest, hard-working and really pretty smart, but for some strange reason he could never find a job. He always seemed to get things wrong at interviews. So most of the time he stayed at home, painting his rooms, and making new curtains, and little knick-knacks to brighten up the place. He worked hard, and he liked his house, even if it was kind of unusual.

Toby's friends all knew that Toby was looking for a job and they were always on the lookout for things he could do. One day, his friend Suzie called to say that the office where she worked was looking for a "spokesperson".

"A 'spokesperson,'" thought Toby. "It's an unusual job, but I think I can do it." He went to his garage and took the wheels off his bicycle. Then he went to all his friends and borrowed their bicycle wheels, too. By lunchtime he had lots of wheels and hundreds of spokes. He went to the company and said:

"I'm very good with spokes! See? I've got long ones, short ones, bent ones, but most of them are straight."

The interviewer scratched his head and laughed. "No, a 'spokesperson' is someone who talks to people—newspapers, radio, and television. They tell them what the company does. It's got nothing to do with bicycle wheels."

"Oh," said Toby, and he went home again and made a new coffee table out of a big drainpipe.

The next day, Toby's friend Sam came by to say that the school down the block was looking for

Then a big tornado
Whirled over the sea.
It blew Wendy upwards
As high as could be.

"What a wonderful feeling!"
The whale cried in glee.
"I am floating above
The sparkling blue sea."

The hot-air balloonist
Took her for a spin.
She chatted to sea birds
And waved her huge fin.

He dropped her back home
At the end of the day.
"Oh, thank you!" she smiled,
And then swam away.

Good Homes Wanted

"**M**eow, meow!" A large black-and-white cat sat on the fence outside number three Cherry Tree Avenue, watching and waiting. At exactly four o'clock a schoolboy appeared on the corner of the road and the cat arched its back and purred excitedly as its friend approached.

"Hello, cat," said the boy, whose name was Danny. "Been waiting long?"

"Meow, meow," replied the cat, which meant "Since ten-thirty this morning."

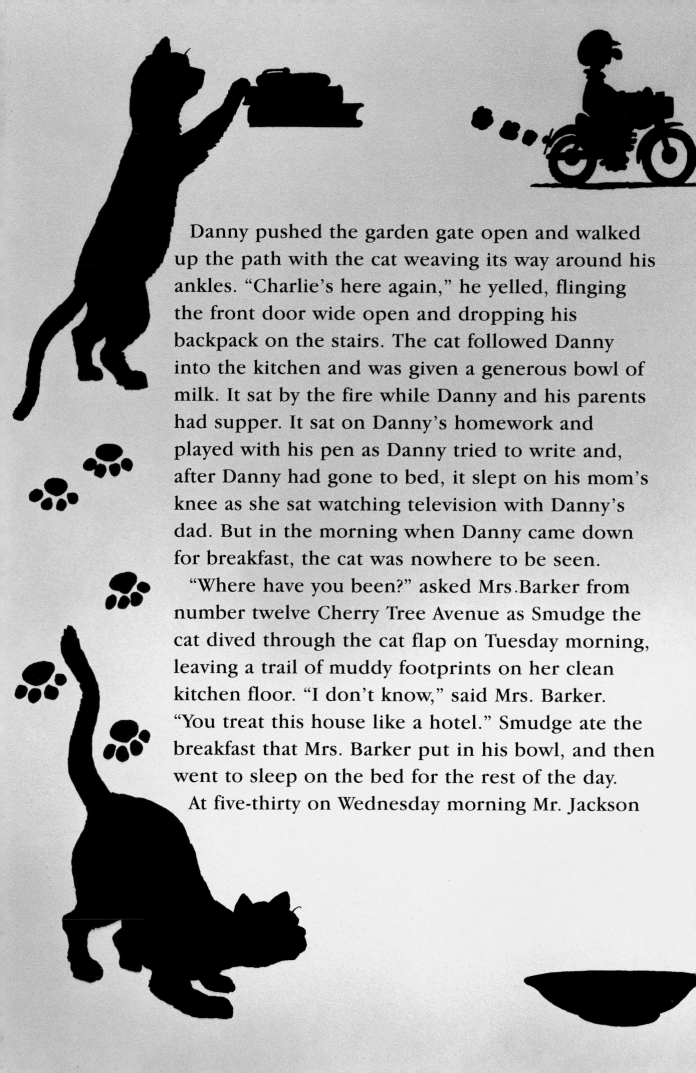

Danny pushed the garden gate open and walked up the path with the cat weaving its way around his ankles. "Charlie's here again," he yelled, flinging the front door wide open and dropping his backpack on the stairs. The cat followed Danny into the kitchen and was given a generous bowl of milk. It sat by the fire while Danny and his parents had supper. It sat on Danny's homework and played with his pen as Danny tried to write and, after Danny had gone to bed, it slept on his mom's knee as she sat watching television with Danny's dad. But in the morning when Danny came down for breakfast, the cat was nowhere to be seen.

"Where have you been?" asked Mrs. Barker from number twelve Cherry Tree Avenue as Smudge the cat dived through the cat flap on Tuesday morning, leaving a trail of muddy footprints on her clean kitchen floor. "I don't know," said Mrs. Barker. "You treat this house like a hotel." Smudge ate the breakfast that Mrs. Barker put in his bowl, and then went to sleep on the bed for the rest of the day.

At five-thirty on Wednesday morning Mr. Jackson

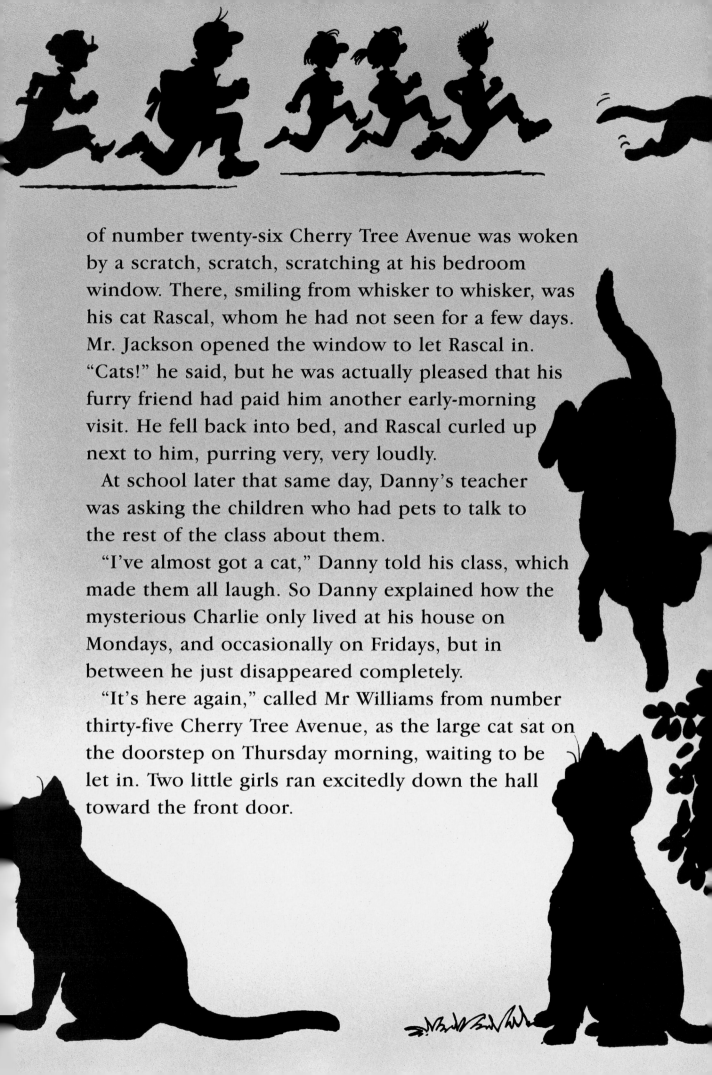

of number twenty-six Cherry Tree Avenue was woken
by a scratch, scratch, scratching at his bedroom
window. There, smiling from whisker to whisker, was
his cat Rascal, whom he had not seen for a few days.
Mr. Jackson opened the window to let Rascal in.
"Cats!" he said, but he was actually pleased that his
furry friend had paid him another early-morning
visit. He fell back into bed, and Rascal curled up
next to him, purring very, very loudly.

At school later that same day, Danny's teacher
was asking the children who had pets to talk to
the rest of the class about them.

"I've almost got a cat," Danny told his class, which
made them all laugh. So Danny explained how the
mysterious Charlie only lived at his house on
Mondays, and occasionally on Fridays, but in
between he just disappeared completely.

"It's here again," called Mr Williams from number
thirty-five Cherry Tree Avenue, as the large cat sat on
the doorstep on Thursday morning, waiting to be
let in. Two little girls ran excitedly down the hall
toward the front door.

"Oh please let him in, Daddy," cried Suzy, the older of the two girls.

"I want to hold him," said Jenny, pushing her sister aside. Mr. Williams tucked his morning paper under one arm. "Now girls, no squabbling, or you'll frighten it," he said. But there was not much chance of that. Mr. Williams opened the door just a little and the cat rushed in, rolling around on the floor enjoying the little girls' attention.

"Can we keep him?" asked Suzy.

"He could sleep on my bed," suggested Jenny helpfully.

"No, mine," insisted Suzy, and another argument broke out.

"Girls, girls," said Mrs Williams, appearing at the top of the stairs in her bathrobe. "Oh, look," she beamed as she spotted the cat. "He's come back. Do you think he'd like some bacon?" The cat rolled onto its back and pedaled an imaginary bicycle, which meant,

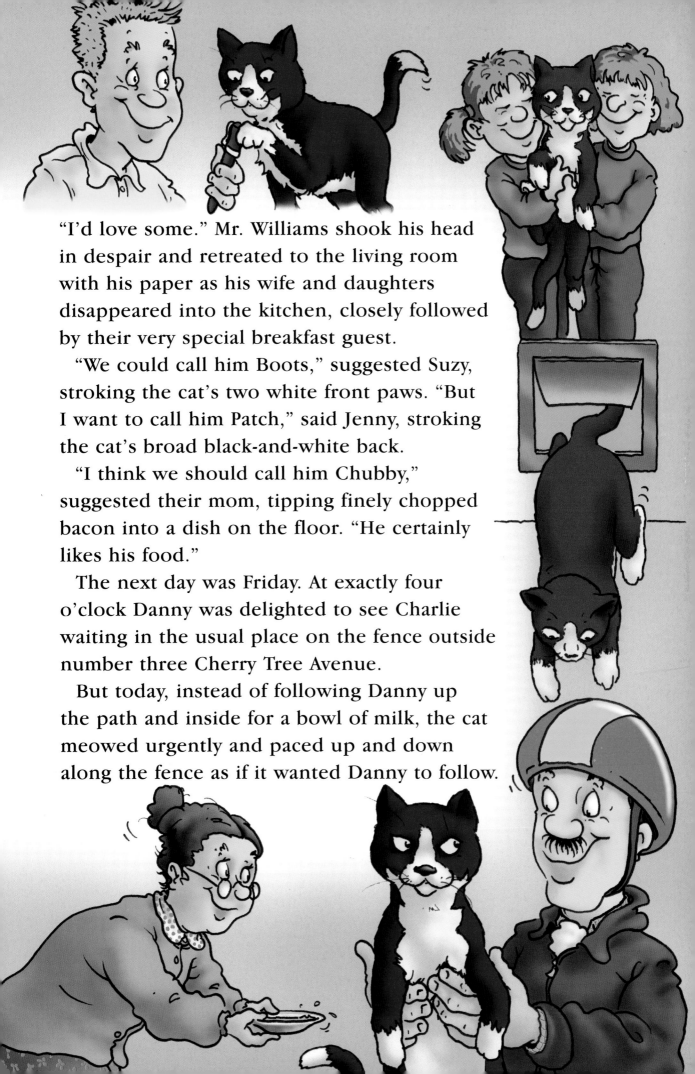

"I'd love some." Mr. Williams shook his head in despair and retreated to the living room with his paper as his wife and daughters disappeared into the kitchen, closely followed by their very special breakfast guest.

"We could call him Boots," suggested Suzy, stroking the cat's two white front paws. "But I want to call him Patch," said Jenny, stroking the cat's broad black-and-white back.

"I think we should call him Chubby," suggested their mom, tipping finely chopped bacon into a dish on the floor. "He certainly likes his food."

The next day was Friday. At exactly four o'clock Danny was delighted to see Charlie waiting in the usual place on the fence outside number three Cherry Tree Avenue.

But today, instead of following Danny up the path and inside for a bowl of milk, the cat meowed urgently and paced up and down along the fence as if it wanted Danny to follow.

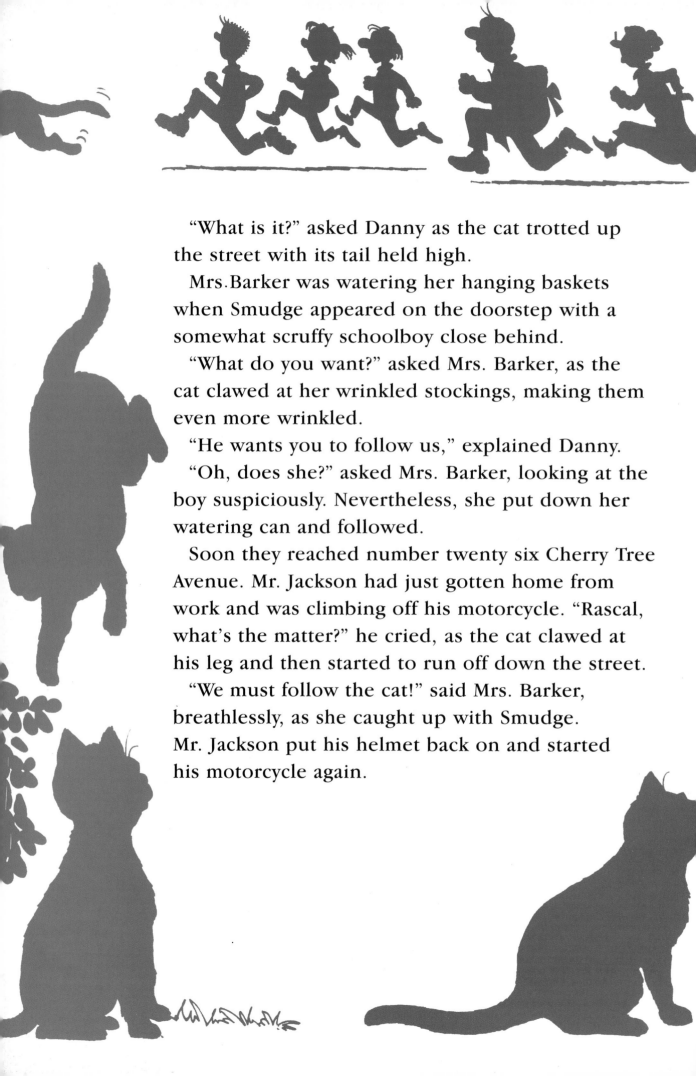

"What is it?" asked Danny as the cat trotted up the street with its tail held high.

Mrs. Barker was watering her hanging baskets when Smudge appeared on the doorstep with a somewhat scruffy schoolboy close behind.

"What do you want?" asked Mrs. Barker, as the cat clawed at her wrinkled stockings, making them even more wrinkled.

"He wants you to follow us," explained Danny.

"Oh, does she?" asked Mrs. Barker, looking at the boy suspiciously. Nevertheless, she put down her watering can and followed.

Soon they reached number twenty six Cherry Tree Avenue. Mr. Jackson had just gotten home from work and was climbing off his motorcycle. "Rascal, what's the matter?" he cried, as the cat clawed at his leg and then started to run off down the street.

"We must follow the cat!" said Mrs. Barker, breathlessly, as she caught up with Smudge. Mr. Jackson put his helmet back on and started his motorcycle again.

He wobbled off after Rascal, with Danny and Mrs. Barker trying desperately to keep up.

"Nyawww," went the bike as it turned the corner into Market Street. "Meow, meow," said the cat as it spotted Mr. Roe the fishseller.

"Well, I never," said Mr. Roe in surprise when he saw the strange line of people trying to keep up with a cat. Curiosity got the better of him, and he thought he had better join them—he might be missing out on something!

The cat then ran through the outdoor market closely followed by Mr. Jackson and Mr. Roe with Danny and poor old Mrs. Barker bringing up the rear.

People gazed in amazement as the cat and its pursuers disappeared around the corner into the playground.

Mrs. Williams was pushing her two daughters on the swings.

"Look, it's Socks!" cried Suzy.

"No, it's Patch," corrected Jenny, and they both jumped off the swings and followed Mr. Jackson, Mr. Roe, Danny and Mrs. Barker, whose stockings were now very, *very* wrinkled!

At last, and much to everyone's relief, the cat stopped. They all looked at each other, feeling slightly awkward and embarrassed, and then they all looked down at the cat. She seemed to be smiling as with her nose she gently made a gap in the hedge to reveal six beautiful black-and-white kittens. Kittens all ready and waiting for their new owners to take them to their purrrrrfect new homes.

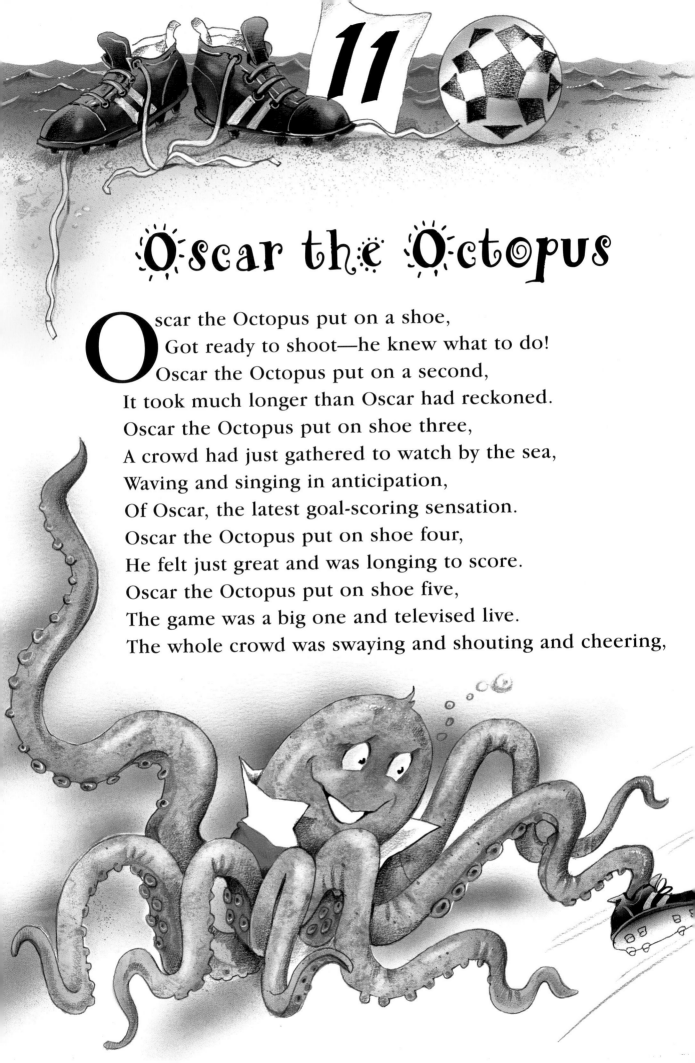

Oscar the Octopus

Oscar the Octopus put on a shoe,
Got ready to shoot—he knew what to do!
Oscar the Octopus put on a second,
It took much longer than Oscar had reckoned.
Oscar the Octopus put on shoe three,
A crowd had just gathered to watch by the sea,
Waving and singing in anticipation,
Of Oscar, the latest goal-scoring sensation.
Oscar the Octopus put on shoe four,
He felt just great and was longing to score.
Oscar the Octopus put on shoe five,
The game was a big one and televised live.
The whole crowd was swaying and shouting and cheering,

And hoping that Oscar would soon be appearing.
Oscar the Octopus put on shoe six,
And stood on his head as he practiced some kicks.
Oscar the Octopus put on shoe seven,
And straightened his jersey—he was number eleven.
He gazed in the mirror and felt really proud,
It was time for his debut in front of the crowd.
Just one more shoe—would he ever be ready?
The laces were tangled, his nerves were unsteady.
Oscar the Octopus put on shoe eight,
Walked onto the field but the Ref said, "Too late.
The game is all over, the whistle has blown,
Nobody scored, and the crowd has gone home."

Steve and Stella

"**G**ive that present to me!" Steve shouted at his sister Stella. "It's much better than mine!" He launched himself angrily at her and made a grab for the model dinosaur she had just been given by Santa Claus, who was sitting in the Christmas display of a big department store. Stella stepped swiftly aside, and Steve crashed straight into a model of Rudolph the Red-Nosed Reindeer, complete with flashing nose. It swayed, then fell, bringing the Christmas tree down, too. Decorations went flying, and waiting children ran away, shrieking, for safety.

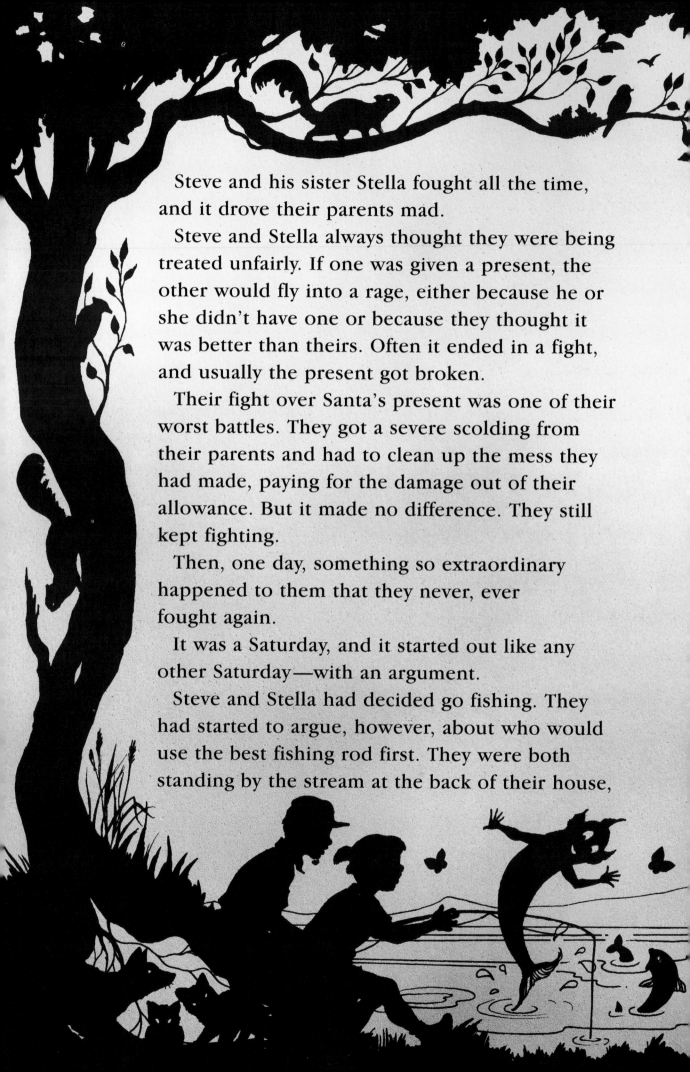

Steve and his sister Stella fought all the time, and it drove their parents mad.

Steve and Stella always thought they were being treated unfairly. If one was given a present, the other would fly into a rage, either because he or she didn't have one or because they thought it was better than theirs. Often it ended in a fight, and usually the present got broken.

Their fight over Santa's present was one of their worst battles. They got a severe scolding from their parents and had to clean up the mess they had made, paying for the damage out of their allowance. But it made no difference. They still kept fighting.

Then, one day, something so extraordinary happened to them that they never, ever fought again.

It was a Saturday, and it started out like any other Saturday—with an argument.

Steve and Stella had decided go fishing. They had started to argue, however, about who would use the best fishing rod first. They were both standing by the stream at the back of their house,

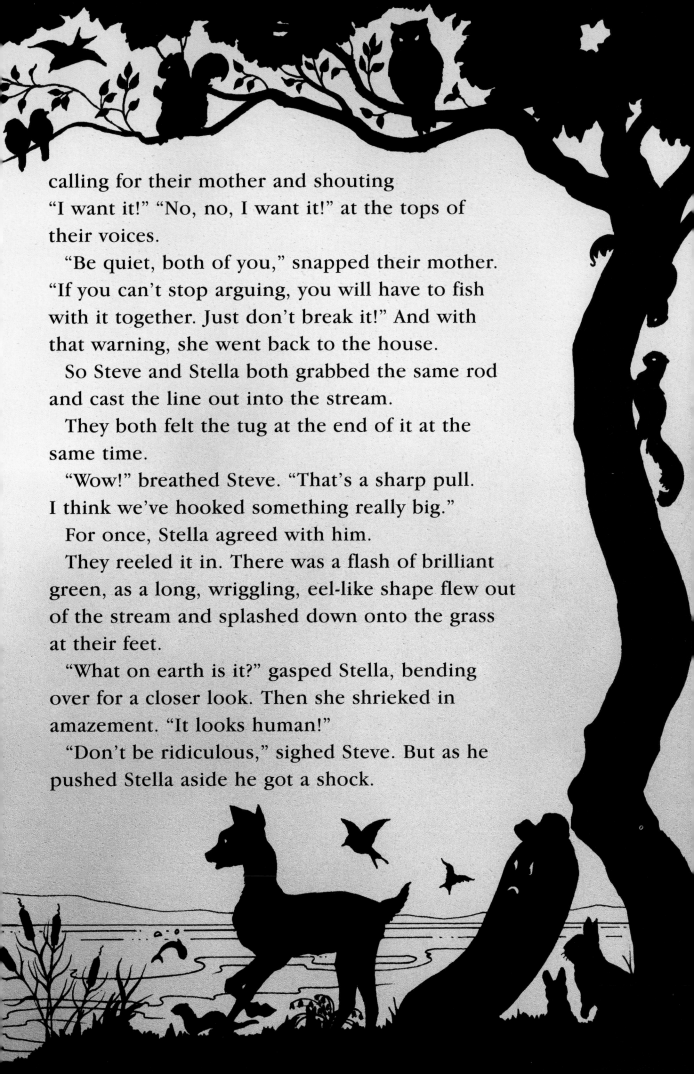

calling for their mother and shouting
"I want it!" "No, no, I want it!" at the tops of
their voices.

"Be quiet, both of you," snapped their mother.
"If you can't stop arguing, you will have to fish
with it together. Just don't break it!" And with
that warning, she went back to the house.

So Steve and Stella both grabbed the same rod
and cast the line out into the stream.

They both felt the tug at the end of it at the
same time.

"Wow!" breathed Steve. "That's a sharp pull.
I think we've hooked something really big."

For once, Stella agreed with him.

They reeled it in. There was a flash of brilliant
green, as a long, wriggling, eel-like shape flew out
of the stream and splashed down onto the grass
at their feet.

"What on earth is it?" gasped Stella, bending
over for a closer look. Then she shrieked in
amazement. "It looks human!"

"Don't be ridiculous," sighed Steve. But as he
pushed Stella aside he got a shock.

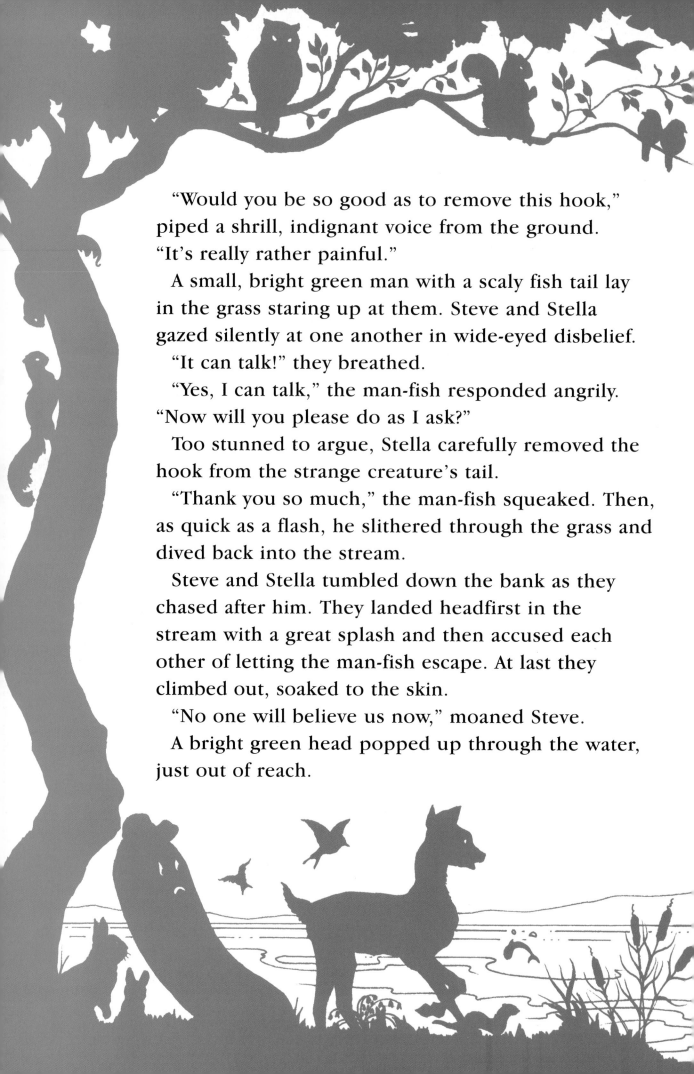

"Would you be so good as to remove this hook," piped a shrill, indignant voice from the ground. "It's really rather painful."

A small, bright green man with a scaly fish tail lay in the grass staring up at them. Steve and Stella gazed silently at one another in wide-eyed disbelief.

"It can talk!" they breathed.

"Yes, I can talk," the man-fish responded angrily. "Now will you please do as I ask?"

Too stunned to argue, Stella carefully removed the hook from the strange creature's tail.

"Thank you so much," the man-fish squeaked. Then, as quick as a flash, he slithered through the grass and dived back into the stream.

Steve and Stella tumbled down the bank as they chased after him. They landed headfirst in the stream with a great splash and then accused each other of letting the man-fish escape. At last they climbed out, soaked to the skin.

"No one will believe us now," moaned Steve.

A bright green head popped up through the water, just out of reach.

"I almost forgot," the man-fish called to them. "I grant you three wishes for catching me and then letting me go."

He disappeared beneath the water and was never seen again.

Steve and Stella looked at one another. Were they dreaming? Had they really been granted three wishes?

"I've read about this kind of thing in fairy stories," said Steve doubtfully. "But everyone knows that's all make-believe."

"Well, it can't be make-believe, can it?" Stella retorted. "What about the little green man? He was a fairy tale creature all right."

Steve agreed that they had actually hooked a creature that could talk and was half man and half fish. "But I bet you're wrong about the wishes," he scoffed.

"That's fine with me, Mr. Know-It-All," sneered Stella. "I'll take all three wishes. Now, what should I wish for first?"

"Oh no, you don't," said Steve, hurriedly putting a hand over her mouth to stop her.

Furious, Stella struggled away and tried to stop Steve from speaking. He pushed her away roughly, making her even more angry. Before they knew it, they had started fighting and the wishes went straight out of their heads.

Eventually, exhausted and feeling cold and hungry, Steve and Stella stopped fighting and flung themselves down on the grass.

"I'm starving!" complained Steve. "I wish I had a giant sausage to eat!"

There was a flash of bright green light, and an enormous, delicious-smelling fried sausage appeared, right beside him.

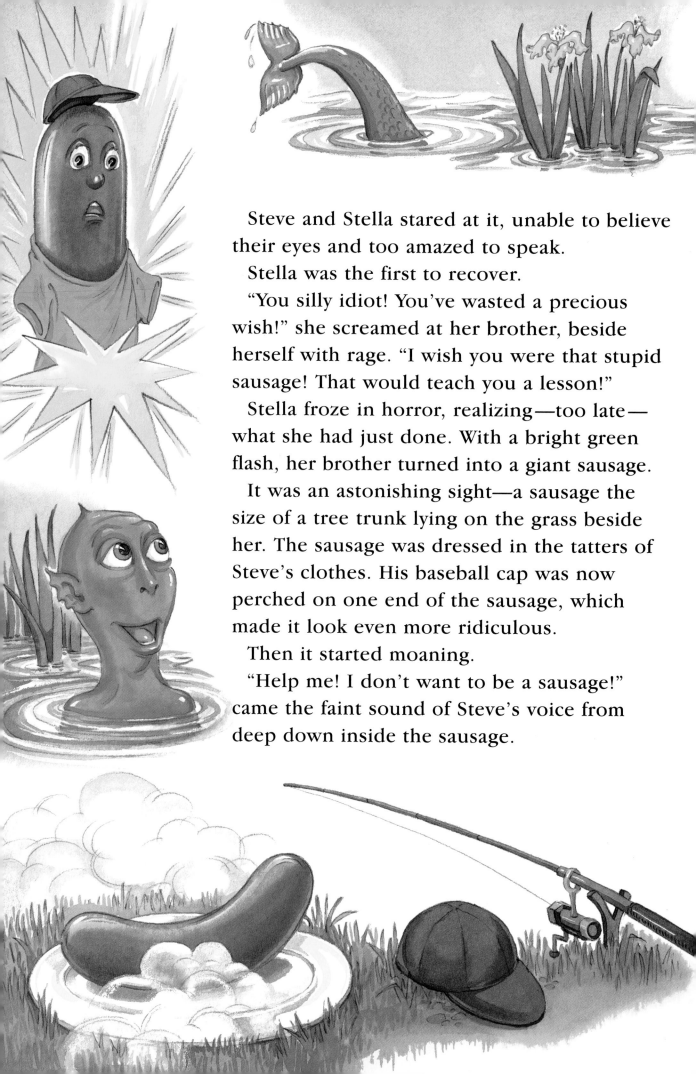

Steve and Stella stared at it, unable to believe their eyes and too amazed to speak.

Stella was the first to recover.

"You silly idiot! You've wasted a precious wish!" she screamed at her brother, beside herself with rage. "I wish you were that stupid sausage! That would teach you a lesson!"

Stella froze in horror, realizing—too late— what she had just done. With a bright green flash, her brother turned into a giant sausage.

It was an astonishing sight—a sausage the size of a tree trunk lying on the grass beside her. The sausage was dressed in the tatters of Steve's clothes. His baseball cap was now perched on one end of the sausage, which made it look even more ridiculous.

Then it started moaning.

"Help me! I don't want to be a sausage!" came the faint sound of Steve's voice from deep down inside the sausage.

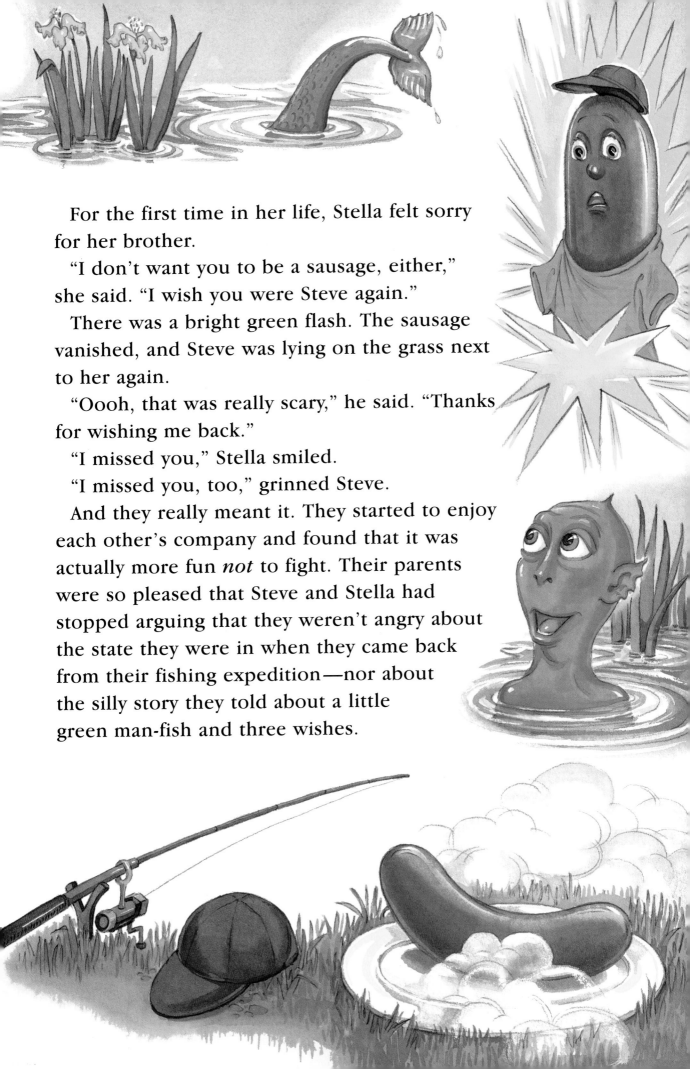

For the first time in her life, Stella felt sorry for her brother.

"I don't want you to be a sausage, either," she said. "I wish you were Steve again."

There was a bright green flash. The sausage vanished, and Steve was lying on the grass next to her again.

"Oooh, that was really scary," he said. "Thanks for wishing me back."

"I missed you," Stella smiled.

"I missed you, too," grinned Steve.

And they really meant it. They started to enjoy each other's company and found that it was actually more fun *not* to fight. Their parents were so pleased that Steve and Stella had stopped arguing that they weren't angry about the state they were in when they came back from their fishing expedition—nor about the silly story they told about a little green man-fish and three wishes.

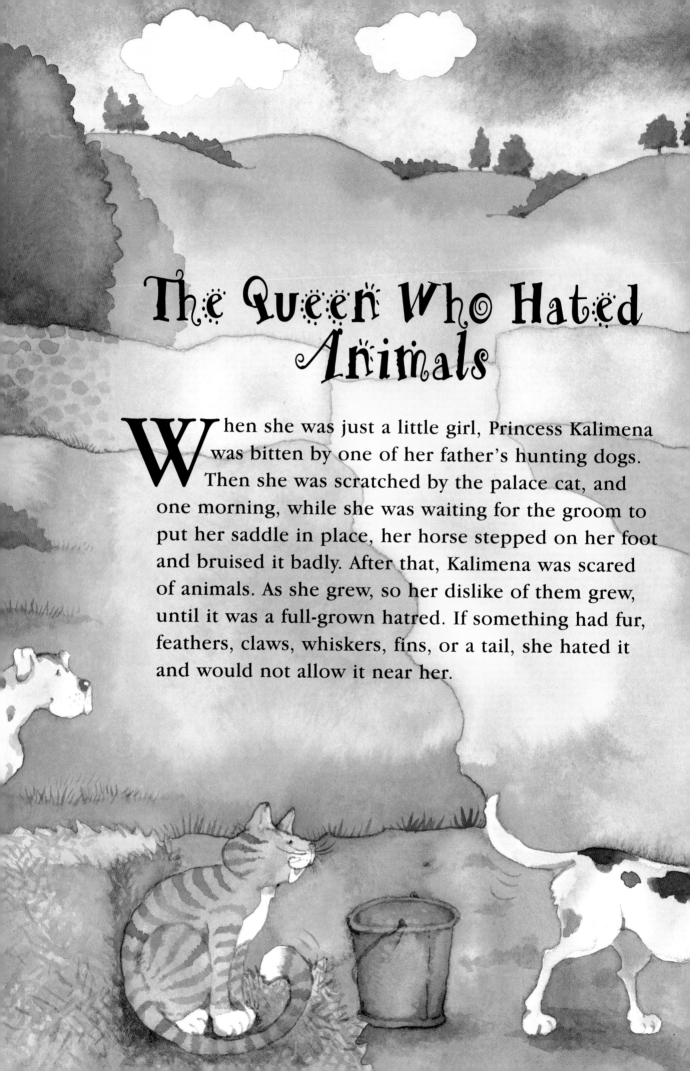

The Queen Who Hated Animals

When she was just a little girl, Princess Kalimena was bitten by one of her father's hunting dogs. Then she was scratched by the palace cat, and one morning, while she was waiting for the groom to put her saddle in place, her horse stepped on her foot and bruised it badly. After that, Kalimena was scared of animals. As she grew, so her dislike of them grew, until it was a full-grown hatred. If something had fur, feathers, claws, whiskers, fins, or a tail, she hated it and would not allow it near her.

So when Princess Kalimena became Queen Kalimena, the first thing she did was pass a very unpopular new law.

"From this day forth, all animals are banned from the land," she declared.

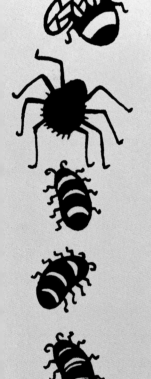

Now, this was not too difficult to do in the palace grounds. The horses were removed from their stables, the dogs were taken out of their cozy kennels, and the peacocks were banished from the gardens. But the servants in the palace had a terrible time. Spiders were brushed from the corners, shutters were closed against stray bees, but no matter what they did, pill bugs always found a way in.

Out in the kingdom, it was even harder to banish the animals. The people needed their sheep and pigs, and their cows and chickens, and they loved their pets. And how could they possibly banish the birds and snakes, butterflies and rabbits? It was a silly law made by a silly queen, they thought.

However, silly as she was, the queen was very powerful and had to be obeyed. So the people found

have tangled hair, don't you, Your Majesty?"

"Indeed," said the queen, eyeing Tasha suspiciously. "Is there any pepper?" she asked.

"Here, Your Majesty," said Tasha, placing her pet hamster in front of the queen. Hammie was wearing a little hat full of pepper with holes in the top, and he was standing as still and upright as he could, with his eyes closed.

"What a strange-looking pepper shaker," said the queen, picking up Hammie and shaking him vigorously. A cloud of pepper filled the room and Hammie sneezed.

"It sneezed!" cried the queen in alarm. "I am sure the pepper shaker sneezed!"

Then one of the rabbits moved. It wasn't his fault; the heavy books were leaning against him. As books tumbled off the shelf the rabbit leaped out of the way to avoid being squashed.

The queen screamed and turned to Tasha, her face red with rage.

"You know I have banned animals!" she yelled, and stamped her foot hard, right on the kangaroo's foot. That was enough for the poor kangaroo. He started bounding around the room, with the queen holding on for dear life. Squealing loudly, the pig ran off and the plates fell crashing to the floor. The cranes squawked and took off out the window, the lampshades still on their heads. The cat cushions leaped from the chairs, the snake draft stoppers slithered out the door, and the kangaroo bounded out of the house and made for the open country, with Queen Kalimena still clinging to him.

"Put me down!" screamed the queen, and finally the kangaroo did—but just then the swans decided it was time to get away.

They flapped their wings and took to the

air, taking the queen with them as they flew. Higher and higher they soared.

"OHHH!" screamed the queen. Then "Oohh," in a slightly different voice. She was flying, which was something she'd always wanted to do. The swans took her high over her kingdom, beating their great white wings, and the queen laughed as she swooped low over the palace and the town. When the swans finally brought the queen gently down beside the lake, she was ecstatic.

Her court officials ran outside.

"Shoot the swans," one of them shouted.

"No," cried the queen. "Let them live. Let all the animals live. They are wonderful."

So the swans returned to the lake, the rabbits went back to their burrows, the sheep climbed gratefully down from the trees, and they all lived properly ever after.

Ice Cool Duel

Angelino's Famous Ice Cream
Has a rival in the town,
A juggling ice cream man called Bob,
Who'll bring his business down.

Bob, who's really a nice fellow,,
Says, "Angelino, don't move out.
We'll have a juggling contest,
And the winner keeps the route."

Bob's talent is impressive,
Though his ice cream tastes like soap.
Poor Angelino, no performer,
Doesn't think he has a hope.

A crowd soon gathers on the sidewalk,
Two small children keep the scores.
Bob twirls a triple-dipper,
To a ripple of applause.

Angelino keeps his cool, though,
Knows that he will be just fine.
What goes up a plain old cone,
Comes down a lemon'n' lime.

Bob hates the thought of losing,
Reaches down toward his knees,
Pulls out a cherry-flavored ice pop,
Tells Angelino, "Time to *freeze*!"

But Angelino's wise to Bob,
So he plays his final trick.
Bob falls, knocked out cold,
By a large vanilla brick!

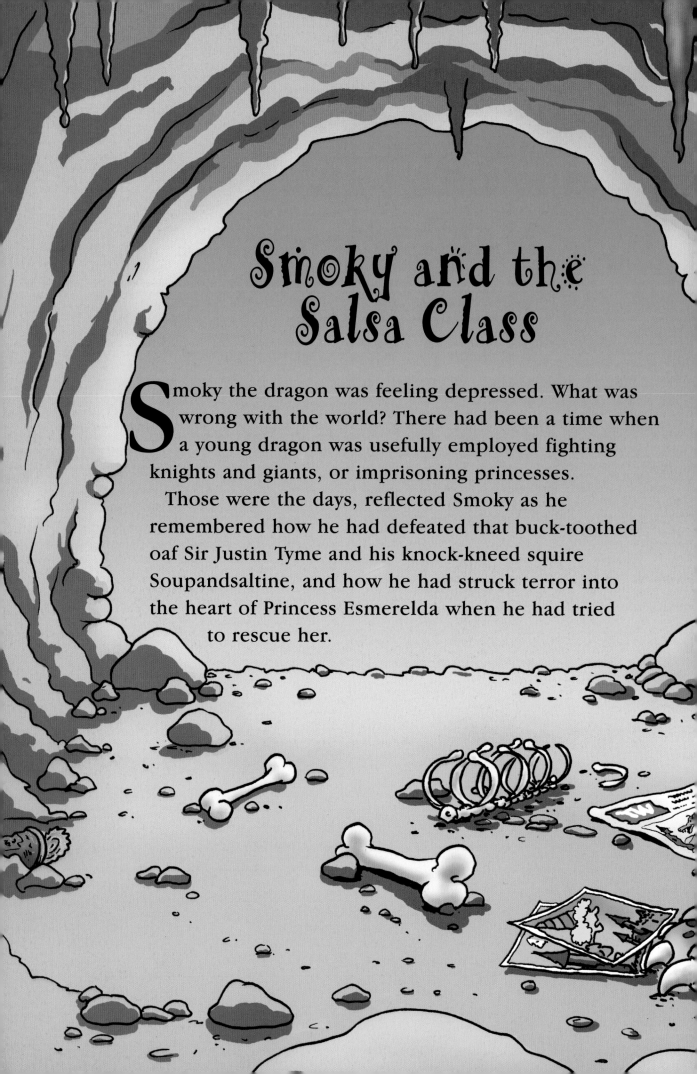

Smoky and the Salsa Class

Smoky the dragon was feeling depressed. What was wrong with the world? There had been a time when a young dragon was usefully employed fighting knights and giants, or imprisoning princesses.

Those were the days, reflected Smoky as he remembered how he had defeated that buck-toothed oaf Sir Justin Tyme and his knock-kneed squire Soupandsaltine, and how he had struck terror into the heart of Princess Esmerelda when he had tried to rescue her.

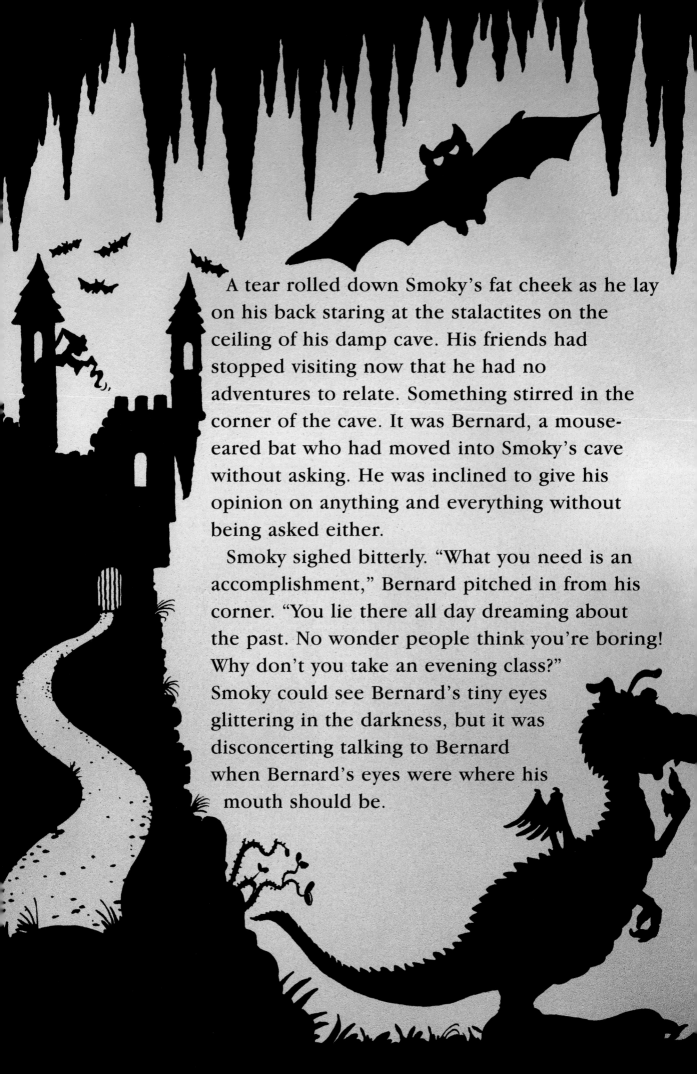

A tear rolled down Smoky's fat cheek as he lay on his back staring at the stalactites on the ceiling of his damp cave. His friends had stopped visiting now that he had no adventures to relate. Something stirred in the corner of the cave. It was Bernard, a mouse-eared bat who had moved into Smoky's cave without asking. He was inclined to give his opinion on anything and everything without being asked either.

Smoky sighed bitterly. "What you need is an accomplishment," Bernard pitched in from his corner. "You lie there all day dreaming about the past. No wonder people think you're boring! Why don't you take an evening class?" Smoky could see Bernard's tiny eyes glittering in the darkness, but it was disconcerting talking to Bernard when Bernard's eyes were where his mouth should be.

I think I'm in love with the witch," he added.

"Yes, yes," snapped Bernard impatiently. "But what about the salsa dancing?"

"Oh, the dancing," said Smoky sheepishly. "I wasn't very good at it. My big feet, you see. But they're having an end-of-term barbecue," he continued and started to grin. "And I'm certainly going to set that on fire!"

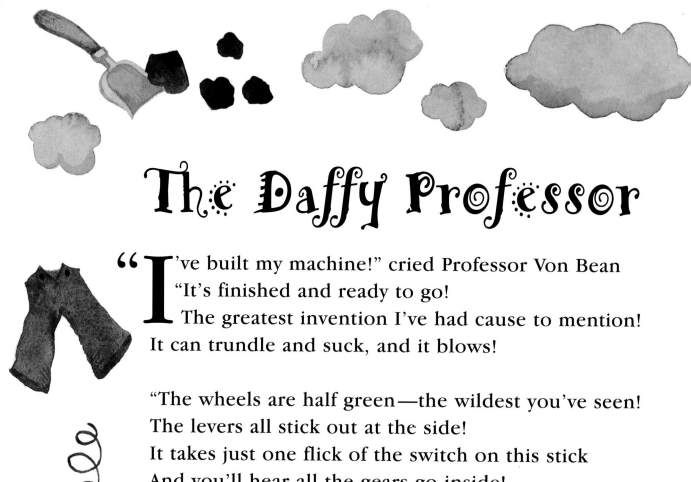

The Daffy Professor

"I've built my machine!" cried Professor Von Bean
"It's finished and ready to go!
The greatest invention I've had cause to mention!
It can trundle and suck, and it blows!

"The wheels are half green—the wildest you've seen!
The levers all stick out at the side!
It takes just one flick of the switch on this stick
And you'll hear all the gears go inside!

"It's got bright red stripes and lots of weird pipes
And things that light up on on the roof!
The coal goes in here and the smoke goes out there,
And instead of 'toot', it goes 'woof'!

"The door's made of glass, and the floor's made of grass!
There are flowers and plants on the back!
There's a cupboard inside that's really quite wide,
So there's somewhere to store a snack!"

Von Bean was delighted and very excited
And happily burst into song.
But his assistant was flustered and suddenly blustered,
"I think that something is wrong!"

"I know I'm persistent!" cried Von Bean's young assistant
"And I love your machine through and through!
The lights flash on top when it spins and can't stop!
But what on earth does it DO?"

With a terrible cry and a long, drawn-out sigh,
Von Bean said, "Oh what a fool!
I never once thought — I've really been caught —
This machine does *nothing useful at all*!"

The Flying Contest

It was a hot day on the African savannah when the animals saw that a sign had been tacked to the trunk of a tree. They gathered around to read it.

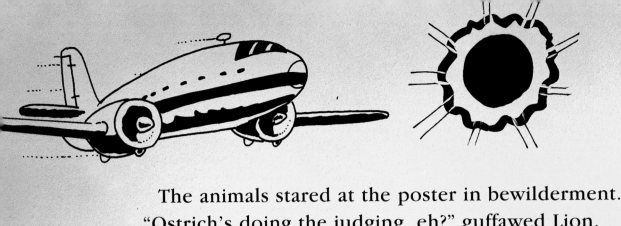

The animals stared at the poster in bewilderment. "Ostrich's doing the judging, eh?" guffawed Lion. "What would he know about flying? Why, he can't even fly himself."

Lion's voice was drowned out by the sound of an airplane passing overhead. The animals looked up at the sky, and one by one they began to get ideas about how to build their flying machines.

"What a flying machine needs is a noisy engine," thought Hippo, as he trundled away to the river.

"No flying machine is complete without a tail," thought Giraffe, as she galloped across the plain.

"The most important things on a flying machine are the wings," thought Lion wisely, as he stole away through the grass.

But Ellie the elephant just couldn't imagine how she would possibly make a flying machine. Ellie was dreadfully forgetful, unlike most elephants—and she had already forgotten what an airplane looked like!

"It must have had wings," she thought, 'so I'd better make myself some. Now let me see….' Ellie tried to remember which creatures she knew that

could escape, she felt herself being
lifted up in the tablecloth and carried high
above the trees. She struggled to free herself
and got all tangled up in the string.

Just then, the other animals felt the gust, too.
They looked up into the sky and stared in
amazement. They couldn't believe their eyes!
Ellie was floating down toward them with the
tablecloth and string acting as a parachute!

"Ellie, you're the winner!" announced Ostrich,
as she landed on the ground with a soft bump.
The other animals cheered and cheered. "It's
time to claim your prize—bring out the balloon
basket!" called Ostrich. Ellie tried to squeeze
her large frame into the basket, but it just
wouldn't fit.

"I'd miss you all anyway," she said. "Why don't
we have a picnic together instead? It just so
happens that I'm still hungry!" So that is exactly
what they all did.

The Singing Bank Robber

Bernie McTavish had had a bad day at the office. He hadn't really gotten anything done all day. Then his wife phoned to say that a pipe had burst under the hall floor. Everything was all right, but he would have to climb in through the window, because the furniture was in front of the door.

Bernie put the telephone down with a sigh and put on his black leather motorcycle gear. He couldn't see the bag he usually put his office clothes in, so he found an empty cash bag in the safe and stuffed them into that instead.

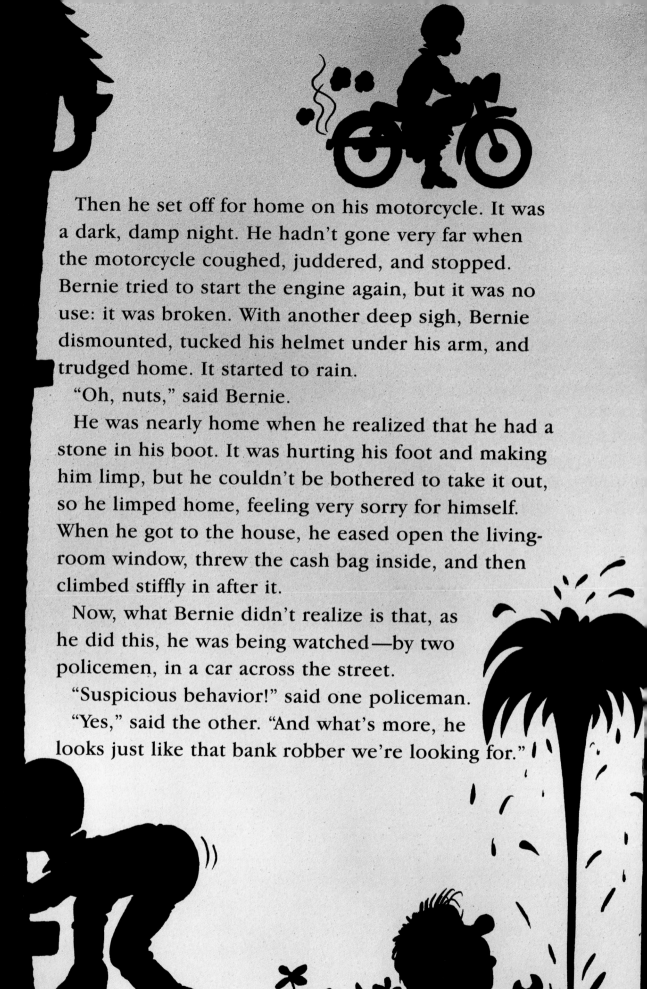

Then he set off for home on his motorcycle. It was a dark, damp night. He hadn't gone very far when the motorcycle coughed, juddered, and stopped. Bernie tried to start the engine again, but it was no use: it was broken. With another deep sigh, Bernie dismounted, tucked his helmet under his arm, and trudged home. It started to rain.

"Oh, nuts," said Bernie.

He was nearly home when he realized that he had a stone in his boot. It was hurting his foot and making him limp, but he couldn't be bothered to take it out, so he limped home, feeling very sorry for himself. When he got to the house, he eased open the living-room window, threw the cash bag inside, and then climbed stiffly in after it.

Now, what Bernie didn't realize is that, as he did this, he was being watched—by two policemen, in a car across the street.

"Suspicious behavior!" said one policeman.

"Yes," said the other. "And what's more, he looks just like that bank robber we're looking for."

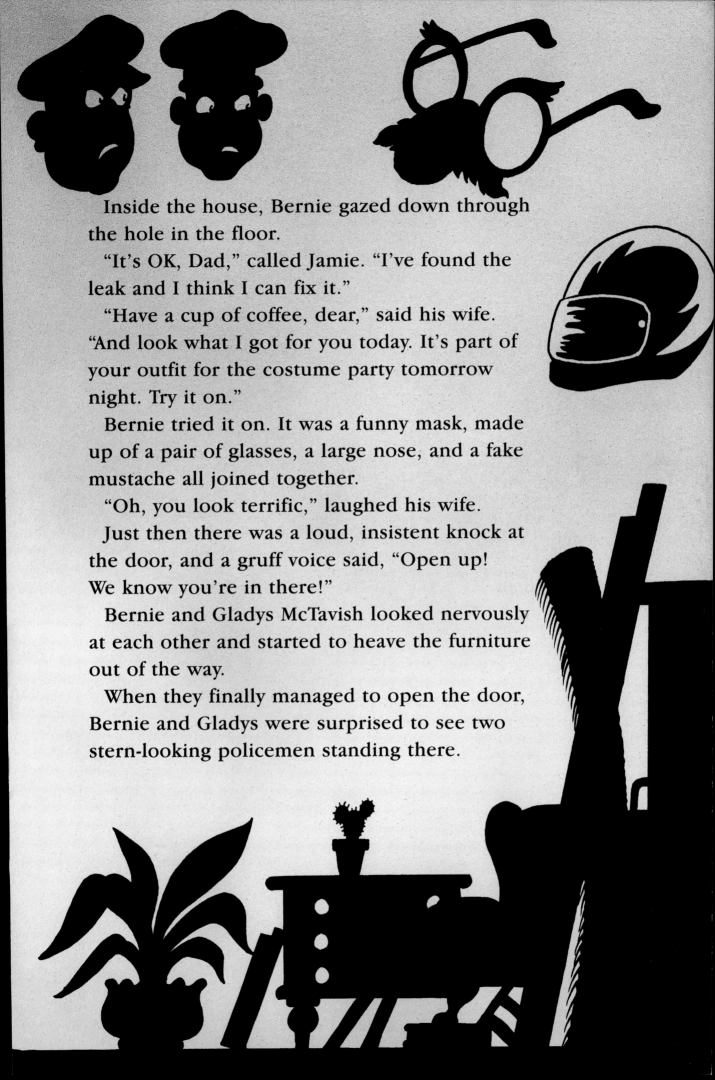

Inside the house, Bernie gazed down through the hole in the floor.

"It's OK, Dad," called Jamie. "I've found the leak and I think I can fix it."

"Have a cup of coffee, dear," said his wife. "And look what I got for you today. It's part of your outfit for the costume party tomorrow night. Try it on."

Bernie tried it on. It was a funny mask, made up of a pair of glasses, a large nose, and a fake mustache all joined together.

"Oh, you look terrific," laughed his wife.

Just then there was a loud, insistent knock at the door, and a gruff voice said, "Open up! We know you're in there!"

Bernie and Gladys McTavish looked nervously at each other and started to heave the furniture out of the way.

When they finally managed to open the door, Bernie and Gladys were surprised to see two stern-looking policemen standing there.

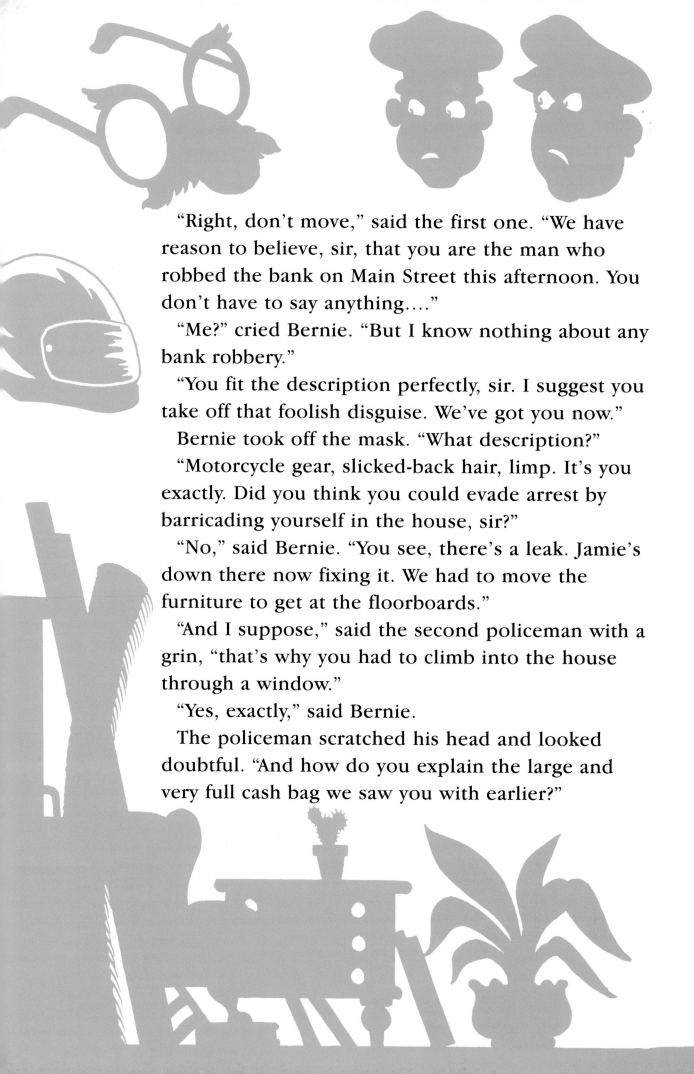

"Right, don't move," said the first one. "We have reason to believe, sir, that you are the man who robbed the bank on Main Street this afternoon. You don't have to say anything...."

"Me?" cried Bernie. "But I know nothing about any bank robbery."

"You fit the description perfectly, sir. I suggest you take off that foolish disguise. We've got you now."

Bernie took off the mask. "What description?"

"Motorcycle gear, slicked-back hair, limp. It's you exactly. Did you think you could evade arrest by barricading yourself in the house, sir?"

"No," said Bernie. "You see, there's a leak. Jamie's down there now fixing it. We had to move the furniture to get at the floorboards."

"And I suppose," said the second policeman with a grin, "that's why you had to climb into the house through a window."

"Yes, exactly," said Bernie.

The policeman scratched his head and looked doubtful. "And how do you explain the large and very full cash bag we saw you with earlier?"

"That was the suit that I wear in the office," said Bernie. "I always change before I come home. And my hair isn't slicked back, it's wet. I got caught in a heavy downpour."

"This all seems very unlikely, sir," said the first policeman. "How do you explain the bowling ball?"

"Bowling ball?"

"The robber threatened to knock over the bank staff with a bowling ball if they didn't hand over the cash. We clearly saw you with a bowling ball tucked under your arm, sir. You can't fool us."

For a moment Bernie didn't know what on earth they were talking about. Then his face brightened.

"Oh, no," he said. "That's not a bowling ball. That's my motorcycle helmet." He showed them the helmet.

"Ah-ha," said the policeman, as if he'd finally found the flaw in Bernie's argument. "But you arrived on foot."

"Yes, my bike broke down," said Bernie. "You see, there's an explanation for everything."

"And the limp?" asked the second policeman, looking more and more puzzled.

"A stone. In my boot," said Bernie. He took off his boot and held it upside-down, and a tiny stone tinkled out onto the floor.

The first policeman whispered something to the second policeman. The second policeman looked doubtful for a moment and then said, "Could you sing for us, sir?"

"Sing?" said Bernie.

"Yes, sing a song for us."

"Anything in particular, Officer?" asked Bernie. He was beginning to think these two policemen were completely mad.

"Something from an opera, sir."

"But I don't know anything from an opera."

"Well, anything will do," said the second policeman.

Bernie took a deep breath and started to sing, "When the red, red, robin comes bob-bob-bobbing along...."

It sounded terrible. Bernie had never been much of a singer. He sounded like a cat stuck in a tree.

"Well, that's it," said the second policeman. "This is the wrong guy. He isn't the bank robber."

"It is?" said the first. "I mean, he isn't?"

"Yes, he isn't."

Everyone looked at the second policeman in complete bewilderment. "Why?" they asked.

"Well, while the staff was filling the cash bag, the robber was singing—something from an opera. And an eyewitness..."

making out a check and handing it over to Mrs. Walker, the woman selling the pups. She smiled broadly. "Well it's the strangest thing. He doesn't bark at all. I don't think he can."

Ben's dad was still shaking his head when the three of them got home.

"A six-inch-high watchdog, with a ridiculous tail, a floppy ear, and no bark," he complained to Ben's mom as she watched Ben and his new best friend race around the yard.

"Well, Ben certainly seems to like him," she remarked. And Ben certainly did.

It didn't take long for the new puppy to settle down. Ben gave him the name Jake, which sort of suited him. Jake was having the time of his life— a comfy new basket, an elegant tartan collar with his name on it, an enormous yard and a wonderful family. He tried very hard to please them all, especially Ben's dad. He handed him the hammer when he was putting the *Beware of the Dog* sign on the gate. He hadn't meant to drop it on his toe, of course, but it was kind of heavy for a small dog.

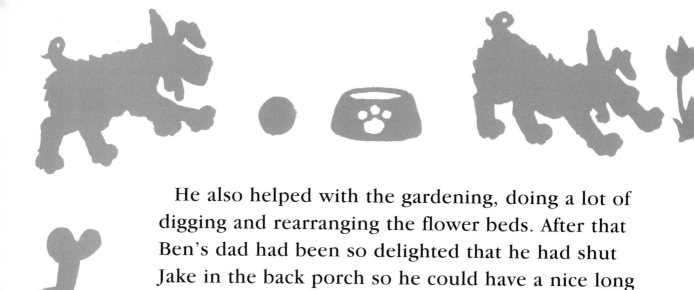

He also helped with the gardening, doing a lot of digging and rearranging the flower beds. After that Ben's dad had been so delighted that he had shut Jake in the back porch so he could have a nice long rest in his basket—digging was hard work, especially when you only had short legs.

And Jake really loved his basket. But, as the weeks rolled by and winter approached, it occurred to him that he might be warmer and even more comfortable if he took his beautiful gray blanket and put it on the living room sofa—after all, Ben's dad spent many a happy hour there.

It wasn't easy dragging the heavy blanket down the hall, but eventually he got there—just in time to see two men climbing in through the lounge window.

"Hey, they've got a dog," said the first man, whose name was Stan, as he shone a flashlight in Jake's bewildered face.

"That would explain the sign on the gate," replied the second man, whose name was Eric, as he tumbled headfirst through the window.

"What sign?" asked Stan, who could not read.

I wish I was a dolphin,
A dolphin would be my wish.
Leaping and splashing, I'd be very dashing,
And swim along with the fish.

I wish I was an ostrich,
An ostrich would be grand.
But if I got scared, would I be prepared
To bury my head in the sand?

I wish I had more wishes,
But now my game is through,
I'm happy to be, quite simply me,
Enjoying a day at the zoo.

Madame Monocle's Magic Machine

It was the king's birthday, and Quentin the royal bard had spent days preparing a birthday poem of immense length for His Royal Highness. He had searched the royal library for the perfect rhyme, for the right adjective, for the words that were guaranteed to bring His Majesty pleasure.

At last the ink was dry and Quentin was ready to read his poem to the king. The court assembled, the king took his place upon his throne, and Quentin cleared his throat and began.

"To you, dear Majesty, on the auspicious occasion of your birthday…"

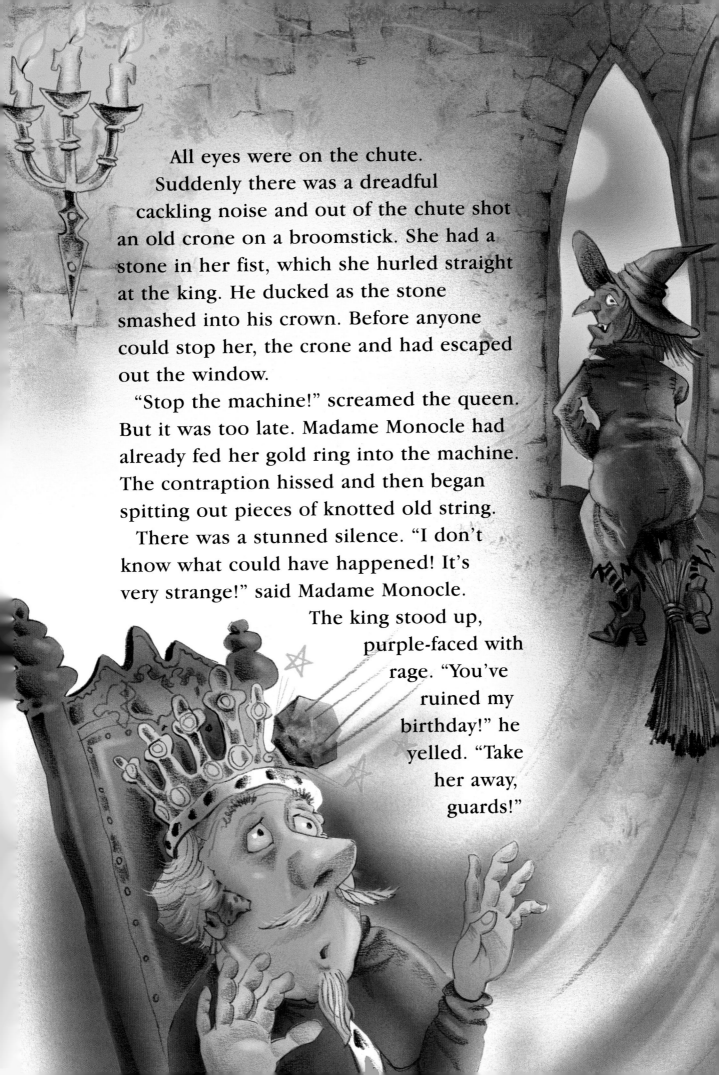

All eyes were on the chute.
Suddenly there was a dreadful
cackling noise and out of the chute shot
an old crone on a broomstick. She had a
stone in her fist, which she hurled straight
at the king. He ducked as the stone
smashed into his crown. Before anyone
could stop her, the crone and had escaped
out the window.

"Stop the machine!" screamed the queen.
But it was too late. Madame Monocle had
already fed her gold ring into the machine.
The contraption hissed and then began
spitting out pieces of knotted old string.

There was a stunned silence. "I don't
know what could have happened! It's
very strange!" said Madame Monocle.

The king stood up,
purple-faced with
rage. "You've
ruined my
birthday!" he
yelled. "Take
her away,
guards!"

"Wait!" shouted the queen. "I know your game," she continued, pointing her finger at Quentin, who was smirking in the corner. "Bone, crone, stone! Ring, string! Obviously our precious court poet has turned the machine into a ridiculous rhymer!"

"Bring him here!" commanded the king. The guards, who had Madame Monocle in a tight grip, dropped their hold. They surrounded Quentin and dragged him in front of the king.

"Well?" demanded the king.

At first Quentin denied everything. But at last he had to admit that he had tampered with the machine. He told the king how hurt he was that no one had wanted to listen to his poem.

The king looked thoughtful. He whispered something to the queen, who thought for a moment and then nodded. Finally, he said to Quentin, "Although you have greatly displeased us, nevertheless the queen and I are forced to admire your skill at producing rhymes out of this machine. As punishment, you will feed it your own work, and we'll see what comes out!"

Reluctantly, Quentin fed sheet after sheet of his poem into the machine. After much whirring, down the chute came a scrap of paper with a few lines of writing on it. Quentin picked it up.

"Well?" said the king.

"It's not quite what I would have liked…." said Quentin hesitantly.

"Let's hear it anyway!" retorted the king.
Quentin arched his eyebrows and read:

There once was a young king named Reggie
Who liked cakes more than meat and two veggies
He declared, "It's a fluke
That greens make me puke,
And chops make me nervous and edgy!"

The king looked surprised. Then he burst out
laughing, and so did the entire court. "Excellent!"
he cried. "I love it! But speaking of cakes—where's
my birthday cake?"

There was an awkward silence in court. Then Madame Monocle stepped forward.

"Perhaps I can help," she said, as she fed a box of matches into the machine. Presto—out came a chocolate cake with candles blazing on it!

"My best birthday ever!" beamed the king, as he blew out his candles.

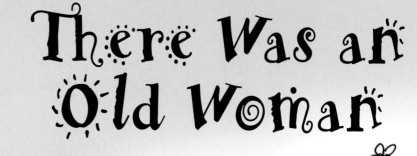

There Was an Old Woman

There was an old woman
Who lived on our street.
You wouldn't believe all
The things she could eat.

For breakfast each morning,
A full three-course meal
Of nuts and bolts served in
A bicycle wheel!

She always was careful
Not to miss lunch.
On brooms, mops, and buckets
She'd nibble and crunch.

Trumpets and trombones were
Her favorite dinner,
But though always eating,
She kept getting thinner.

At midnight she'd snack on
Some bees in their hives,
All swiftly washed down with
The forks, spoons, and knives!

What would finish her off
No one could have known—
For that nutty, old woman
Choked on a fish bone!